Bismillah

THE KHATAM

Papatia Feauxzar

A RAMADAN LOVE SERIES

Dallas, Texas

1

Copyright

For information contact:

DJARABI KITABS PUBLISHING

PO BOX 703733

DALLAS, TX 75370

www.djarabikitabs.com

Cover Design Concept by Papatia Feauxzar
ISBN-13: 978-1-947148-77-2
Category & Genre: Muslim Romance
First Print Edition: February 2025
10 9 8 7 6 5 4 3 2 1

"The Mumin is a Lover." — Prophet ﷺ

Table of Contents

BOOK ONE: THE CODEX

Chapter 1

☪

Hajaratu

HAJARATU SURVEYED THE ROOM filled with colleagues from the paper and pulp industry, sales representatives, and the likes who had mostly flew in the same day or the day before. She arrived very early in the morning and had time to rest before the night's gala. The room glimmered and her shining black dress was just right. She didn't mix business with pleasure but the fleeting thought of meeting the right love interest crossed her mind. She shot the idea down even though her chances at such an event were higher since the event was taking place in Indonesia; a top producer of paper products. Being a printer herself and a reseller of raw materials related to the industry, she decided to attend the gala to network even though most of the guests were targeted by the organizer to donate funds for ecofriendly efforts. That way she could achieve her charity goals of donating and meet new prospective clients. The soft chatter around Hajaratu jolted her to action, so finally she inched her heeled right foot across the threshold of the room. An attendant greeted her and helped her find her seat.

She read the name facing the seat; *Hajaratu Hilal AbouBouakai.*

"Interesting name," she heard over shoulder.

Hajaratu flipped her veiled head around to look at the person. She squinted her kohl-lined eyes at him.

"*Assalamu aleikum,* I am Tariq. You made quite an entrance," he said looking back at the entrance of the room with a boyish smile on his face. Pulling himself out of his reverie, "So, I had to find a way to talk to you," he added.

She had noticed a few people assessing her when she entered the room, but they quickly resumed their chats. Some looks lingered a little longer on her glistening brown face, but she dismissed their looks and their assumptions, whether it was amazement and the shock of seeing a Black Muslim woman in this realm or something else. She had outgrown the excitement and discomfort these looks often brought with them. She was desensitized.

"*Wa aleikum salam* Tariq, I am Hajaratu. What brings you to this event?" she asked, ignoring his comments on her appearance. He was average height, with a Nubian nose, a bright smile, and captivating brown eyes. He was good-looking, but she tried her best to remain on guard. Plus, he looked so young. If she let the first person in the room destabilize her and let her mind turn to marriage prospects, she would never find any business prospects in this place! So, she tied her jaw and promised herself to remain professional throughout the exchange.

Without missing a bit, the young man hovering around her table replied, "I am a sales rep. I get the raw materials into small resellers' shops. I am very good at my job *alhamdullilah*." He smiled and paused to fish out a business card that he handed her.

It was with a skeptical eye and a slim hesitating hand that Hajaratu took the card and peered at it.

"Tariq Ahmed," she read aloud. "No middle name, strange." *I like strange,* she said to herself.

"That's me. I have a middle name, but I rarely divulge it," he said in a teasing tone.

Her heart fluttered at the disappointment she felt.

"So, what is it?" she asked, betraying herself. At the realization, she bit her lower lip and squeezed her eyes shut.

"I was hoping you would ask. It's Taheer."

"Are you *pure?*" she shot at him with a challenging look.

Before he could answer, more guests arrived at the table forcing the discussion to abruptly close. "You don't have to answer that question. Nice meeting you, see you around insha'Allah."

"My pleasure. Until we meet again insha'Allah."

She sighed under her breath a bit overwhelmed by her desires and the emotions she was trying to keep at bay. She liked how he looked at her. Somehow, it had been a minute since her *iddah* ended five years ago. She yearned for the touch of a real man. She quickly dismissed the thought of this young man warming her and her bed. *Astaghfirullah*, she said to herself and added a *dua* to Allah ﷻ to protect her from hypocrisy and protect her private parts from wrongful actions.

Aameen, she finished her prayer silently. *The first man in the room talks to you and you lose all acumen of business and networking. Get over yourself and start talking business and sharing your business cards!* she chided herself. But her *nafs* would not let go so easily. *You could have given him your card.* "Don't worry, if it's meant to be, this Hilal—Crescent Moon but *will* find *that* Tariq—Bright Star." She said to herself. *I'm so corny…*she thought, shaking off the intrusive thoughts.

11

For the rest of the night, she partook in bookish games, connected with a few paper suppliers and found some rare manuscript collectors.

Chapter 2

The Katib (The Writer)

LIKE MOST PEOPLE WHO attended the symposium from the day before, Tariq had signed up for a tourist/business package. While on this business trip, the travel agency would take him and other attendees to some notable landmarks of Indonesia. He hoped to see Hajaratu again during these activities. *Fool!* His conscience snapped him out of that reverie, and he enjoyed the sightseeing in Indonesia on the second day of his trip, though she wasn't among the group.

By the third day, Tariq woke up sore from all the walking the day before. The plan for the day was to take them to a rice field. On the same day, Hajaratu's group visited the beautiful lush mountains of Indonesia. The day before, her group had visited the rice fields. They had lunch there provided by the travel agency and received history lessons on the rice fields. Toward the end of the trip, they were prompted to buy different types of rice if they wanted. Hajaratu jumped on the occasion knowing that the type of rice used in her culture for porridge was different than the type of rice used for a main dish, like *riz gras, jollof* rice or *thiep djen*. And the type of rice a poor family used was uniquely different from the type of rice a more affluent family ate.

In Ivory Coast, they had a type of rice called *Deni Ka Cha* meaning "the children are a lot." This rice was the preferred type of rice for poor families because it doubled or tripled in size when cooked, while a type of rice like jasmine rice doesn't grow exponentially when cooked. Another type of rice Hajaratu was familiar with was *Malo Woussou,* parboiled rice. Some people call it "the rice with no taste," but it has its uses and achieves those goals perfectly. Hajaratu's natural passion for rice was quelched during the trip.

On day four, while Tariq's traveling party dived into the national park waters, Hajaratu's group relaxed at an Indonesia beach.

Chapter 3

C☾★

Tariq

DAY FIVE ARRIVED, AND the travel agency arranged a surprise destination for Tariq's group. They were told to dress casually, or they could dress up if they wanted to. As long as they looked "presentable."

At 7:30 p.m., Tariq left his room and took the elevator to the lobby as was instructed on the group chat for his traveling *zumrah*. Some of his group mates were waiting and mingling amongst themselves. Everyone waited for the tour buses and the group leaders to give them the green light to go outside the hotel and board their designated buses.

From the light chatter around him, he gathered guesses at what the surprise could be.

"It could be a surprise trip to a museum!" a person advanced.

"Or an art gallery!" another person countered.

After days of climbing mountains, visiting rice fields, diving in national park waters, and chilling at a beach, Tariq was ready for a night where physical activity was not required.

His belly grumbled, and he gulped. *I hope they will be serving food since we will be missing the dinner served at nine at the hotel restaurant.* He then made his way towards the reception to get a cup of water. A glass water jar was filled with ice cubes, lemon slices, and some mint leaves. He was about to reach for a disposable paper cup when one of his travel buddies stopped him.

"Do you have free water bottles in your room?" a soft woman's voice asked behind him. He recognized the voice because he had seen her many times during the trip. She had a unique southern drawl you couldn't miss.

"Yes?" replied Tariq, pivoting to look at her.

"It's best you get it instead of the local water you are not used to," she added, eyeing the jar suspiciously.

"Good idea, Amber. I will go to my room and grab it now."

"Do you need a walking buddy?" The young raven-haired woman asked, smiling a bit too much.

"No, thanks. You don't have to walk with me to my room to keep me company. I will be quick. I don't want to miss the bus. Neither should you. And it should be here in less than ten minutes," he said and loosened his tie around his neck. Her perfume was overpowering, and her bosom was a bit enhanced in a red low neckline evening dress that hugged her fit body appreciatively. The dress had a long slit that went from the middle of her hip down to her ankle. He had seen how fit she was during the whole trip. He had done his best to lower his gaze every time it accidentally fell on any attractive part of her body barely covered by her sports clothes and gear. And when their eyes met during these times, she winked and smiled brightly at him. He normally turned his gaze away with an embarrassed smile and would utter the *dua* of Prophet Yusuf *aleihi salam; madha Allahi*—May Allah protect me. *Aameen*. His throat was very parched now because she was a bit spectacular and an ember of fire in his eyes. The irony in her name didn't escape him.

"Fine. You don't want to invite me to your room. I have a water bottle here," she said and retrieved a small bottle of water from her ball-shaped dressy clutch.

Tariq thanked her and took the water. He first checked to make sure that the lid was still intact before he ingested the contents of the little bottle of water. She stared at his Adam's apple the whole time, and her dissection of his body made him uncomfortable. Thankfully, his discomfort ended at the buzz of his cell phone. On cue, all the travelers were whipping their phones out of their pockets or bringing them to their faces while others were already bypassing their screens with passcodes and biometrics.

"Please proceed outside. The buses are here." Tariq read.

"Let's go," Amber told him, and he followed her. His eyes immediately fell on her uncovered lower back, and he regretted agreeing to her order. Tariq walked faster to get in front of her. He hoped to move ahead of her or find a guy he could chat with instead of this alluring woman stuck to him at the moment.

Tariq's mood suddenly dipped at the test he faced.

"Are you OK?" she asked, looking at him, perhaps sensing tension in his manners.

"Yeah. Look, I am going to sit with the guys. See you around." And he removed himself from the situation. He sensed her surprise from the widening of her eyes and the slight gap between her thin open lips.

"You are avoiding me." She said quite bluntly and recovering quickly from the unexpected diss.

"It's not you. It's me. Thanks for the water, have a great night."

Before she could reply, he took two more long strides and boarded the bus. Tariq greeted the bus driver with a peace greeting since he was donning a *kufi*. Then, he made a beeline to sit beside a young man who had an empty seat next to him. Tariq had seen him before over the course of the five days, but they had not exactly interacted. *Perhaps that could change*, he thought. *I need a refreshing outlook and change of scenery or mind!*

"Hey man! Is this seat taken?" Tariq asked.

"No, have a seat. I am Sean Parnell," the guy said, offering his hand to shake Tariq's.

"Nice to meet you, Sean. I'm Tariq. Where you from and what do you?" Tariq replied, shaking Sean's right hand.

"I'm American, of course. I'm a writer. I came to network and find a cheaper printer for my children's books. The symposium was a nice get-together and great point of sync for people from all over the industry. Diagonally, vertically, and auxiliary, too."

"I agree. But what are you? A business major, too?" Tariq said, chuckling.

"You can't be a writer, an author, I mean, a member of this huge industry and have no sense of business. It's necessary man."

"Well said," Tariq lauded.

Sean and Tariq made small talk and got to know each other until they arrived at the destination.

"A dinner," Tariq exclaimed with relief more to himself than anyone else.

"More like a buffet set up outside. I'm sure some good food has been brought all the way out to this lovely open green space."

Tariq was admiring the ambience, with the dimmed lights in the trees and plants, but before he could say something, a voice rose above all in a microphone.

"Thank you for choosing Touareg agency for your business and vacation plans. We have planned a nice dinner for all of you tonight as a token of our appreciation. Enjoy, eat, and travel with us again. We vow to make your stay, wherever it is, memorable. To my right, there is a table, you can come and give your much needed testimonials. We appreciate your reviews in advance. Thanks, and have a great evening, dear guests."

There was a round of applause and people started queuing for the buffet lines. Some people, like Tariq and Sean, decided to get their reviews out of the way and then go eat in peace before they forgot while in a food coma.

The two continued chatting when Tariq peeked ahead of the line in front of them and recognized someone. His heart leaped.

For the object of his sudden butterflies, he was willing to bend a bit of his rules of interaction with women, hoping Allah ﷻ would let it slide. *Ya Allah, expand my chest with confidence and untie the knot from my chest so she may give me a chance and understand me. Aameen. My soul recognizes that this woman is a true catch,* he confessed to himself.

Then he asked Sean to help him out. "Man, can you please come with me. I need to talk to someone up ahead in the lines. We will lose our spots but please help a brother out. It's very important."

He sensed a little hesitation in Sean who peeked behind him taking note of the lines growing longer behind them.

"Please, man. I may never get this chance again," Tariq begged. "I rather not speak to her alone."

"Fine, let's go. We can leave a review online I guess."

"Thanks man!"

Chapter 4

The Katib

THEY MADE THEIR way to the front of the lines. She was wearing a simple navy *abaya* and matched her headscarf with light copper pumps. He registered all the details of her simple and elegant look with a quick and effective glance and gave her the greeting of peace.

Focused ahead, she cocked her head to the right side to look for the speaker. She was radiating. The smile on her face simply illuminated her brown face, and he prayed that he was the one who was the source of such happiness. *Fool! You just pulled her up from a conversation.*

"You again...*wa aleikum salam*...How are you, young man?" she asked casually while broadening her smile.

"I am good, thanks. How are you, Sister Hajaratu?"

Before she could answer, Sean spoke.

"Good evening, Ma'am," Sean said and extended his hand. She politely declined and explained that it was not allowed in her faith.

"Oh, I apologize. I hope I didn't offend you," he said very apologetically.

"It's okay. So, Mr. Tariq, to what do I owe this special greeting and visit? Are you trying to cut to the front of the line?"

"Maybe?" Tariq advanced, half-joking.

The ladies around Hajaratu gave them side-eyes and abundantly clicked their tongues. So, he straightened himself and stood a little taller and more confident. His chest suddenly puffed up. "No, I was joking," he added, clearing his throat. "I wanted to greet you since I recognized you. I didn't know you used the same travelling agency as us."

"Me neither, but it's not surprising. You know how one travel agency dominates the pilgrimage industry by reaching out to many other Muslim organizations? This one is a bit like that. It's the right way to do business, I think. Anyway, we are timely again, meeting on the first and last day."

"Any husband and children waiting for you at home when you return?" he asked, smoothly getting to the point.

"Just my niece and my black cat that mostly ignores me. Most of my relatives are in Africa.

How about you?" she asked, amused that her comment about her cat tickled him.

"Only my uncles and aunts. Some friends are waiting for me to play ball and soccer with them. Did you at least achieve all your business goals in this land?"

"Yes, *alhamdullilah*," she replied.

"How about you guys?" she asked Tariq and Sean. While standing as if on a sideline, she inched forward with the rest of her line. People around them were busy in conversations and with their plates, but she was sure some people close to them were eavesdropping. She made sure not to be too inquisitive or too unprofessional with her line of questioning.

The young men both replied in the affirmative and continued chatting with her until it was her turn at the testimonial kiosk. Tariq charmed the older women around Hajaratu to allow the two men to go after the object of his butterflies. The verdict: the older women let it slide. One woman even gave her room number to Sean who was smiling ear-to-ear and didn't decline the scandalous and suggestive invite among hoots from the others, which Hajaratu kept chastising with "shs". "Dear friends! Behave!" But she knew that they were incorrigible. So, she giggled at their boldness.

Sean and Tariq ended up being invited to the table of the older women. While they ate, the night temperature started dropping.

"It's getting nippy in here," she said, sighing that her polyester *abaya* was a bit thin.

"May I?" Tariq asked, pointing at his suit.

"Sure. Either I refuse and get up tomorrow with a cold or I take it and sniffles averted, haha! You are such a sweetheart," she said, accepting the suit jacket he placed around her delicate shoulders, while trying his best not to touch her. Still, she could feel some kind of heat radiating between the small distance separating their skins. They were so close to each other. Hajaratu closed her eyes for a moment as he draped his suit around her shoulders. Then he sat down, and the night continued with the smooth ambiance around.

After dinner and dessert, they naturally slid into a walk around the lovely illuminated open space. Staring deeply into his eyes, she said, "Your wife will be a lucky woman, young man. This is my cue. Good night."

"Wait," he said, trying to spend more time in her peaceful and intelligent company.

"We have broken so many rules here tonight, Tariq. It's best we put a brake on it here. I fear Allah سبحانه و تعالى." That's all she had to say to bring him in line.

"Fine, thank you. Your presence feels like Ramadan. Of course, we never wanted the evening to end. Anyway, good night, Sister Hajar. Safe travels back to the US," Tariq said with a heavy sigh. He boldly shortened her name for the familiarity and spark that grew in a few hours between them.

"Likewise," she replied. "Tell your friend goodbye whenever you meet him after his walk of shame." They both laughed and made their separate ways to their rides.

"So, it felt like Ramadan huh?" she asked, walking away, her back facing him.

"No doubt." He confirmed, walking in the other direction, also not looking at her.

***

On the plane back, Tariq saw Amber and apologized if he came off rude the night of the dinner when he abruptly left her company. "Not at all, you have principles. I respect that. Then, Amber told him that she saw him having "all eyes for a woman who was covered in Muslim garb," and that she had admired the woman who could grab a man's attention with way less skin showing. "She was fond of you." Amber knowingly concluded.

"Really?" Tariq said, taken aback.

"For sure," Amber vouched, holding her carrying-on tightly on her shoulder in the walkway of the airplane.

Tariq smiled wide at that.

"Hope you won't think I was stalking you."

"Were you?" he asked laughing.

"I was curious. It will get it out of my system," she said with a long sigh and proceeded to her seat.

Chapter 5

Tariq

AFTER HIS RETURN TO the states, Tariq resumed his routine. Sundays, he woke up early to jog around his quiet and peaceful gated community. His mind looped around the series of verses that he read at *tahajjud* recently. His Ustadh told him one time that we bring our situation to the Quran as the holy manuscript was revealed for the heart. It talks directly to the heart of the believer. Tariq couldn't agree more. In the wee hours of the night, he never set out to read a particular chapter of his ancient Codex. He simply made his heart sound and opened the holy book allowing it to Divinely fall on the verses he needed at the moment.

From the verses "And we have created you in pairs."— Quran 78:8, he gathered that he needed a wife. The day before, it was the first verse of Surah Nisa that he randomly opened his Quran to. Because he was a Hafiz, he told himself, *I feel like the next verse will be 2:187,* and he laughed to himself. Mostly because of the garment part. Then he remembered that his suit coat had stayed with the remarkable Hajaratu. He smiled at the tender reminiscence. His time with her felt so special, like a Ramadan moment. And as Ramadan was approaching, there was still no qualified prospectives in sight. Even during *sunnah* fasting days, like Monday and Thursday, things looked bleak. *Where are all the good women?* he asked himself. *Ya Allah, please help me find her.*

He continued running until his watch alerted him that the time of *ishraaq* had elapsed and that *duha salat* had started. He glanced at the *hijri* date showing in the *salah* app. It was Rabi 1st, six months to Ramadan.

On Sunday nights, he attended a *seerah* class at his local mosque where the Ustadh highlighted incidents in the life of the Prophet ﷺ; most importantly *Shamail* (his character). Tariq had learned quite a lot in this class. The other programs they had during the week at the Islamic center were also attractive, but he couldn't attend them in person due to his busy work schedule.

The next day, Tariq woke up for *fajr* prayer at 3:30 a.m. since the days were longer in Minnesota during that time of the year. He recited a *dua* upon waking up and headed quickly to the washroom while yawning and stretching his fit and long arms. His room was only lit with a desk lamp. Five minutes later, he was out and changing into a *thobe*. His neat closet was only partly in order. The new batch of clothes he had removed from the dryer still sat in the middle of the closet waiting for him to put them on hangers or fold them like the rest of his polo shirts.

Tariq had earmarked his prayer rug after *isha salat* the day before sleeping, so before standing for praying, he straightened it and went into *sujud* pouring his heart out to his Lord about his worries. Then, he sought protection from Allah ﷻ. "Ya Allah, protect me from all sides from the devil and allow me to accomplish my *tilawah* and *tahajjud* easily. *Aameen.*"

Next, he reached for the Quran lying on his bedside table and opened it to a random page. It fell on Surah al-Asr. He read the whole *surah* and then got up to perform two *rakats*. After the *salams*, he supplicated some more. Then, he performed some *zikr* starting by seeking forgiveness and praising Allah ﷻ. He blessed the Messenger, peace be upon him, then he recited a name of Allah ﷻ a hundred times.

Usually after thirty minutes he was done and then normally headed to his study to write on his project. Having been inspired by the biography of his ancestor Ayuba Suleiman Diallo, who wrote several Qurans by hand,

Tariq decided to challenge himself to do the same to please his Creator, build a deeper connection with the Codex, not simply maintaining a superficial connection. Ultimately, his goal was having the Codex as his companion in this life and the next until Allah ﷻ insha'Allah allowed the crowning of his parents, who he lost in a brutal car crash. His uncles and aunts had done a great job raising him and he has been grateful that he didn't end up in the American foster care system. *Alhamdullilah*.

Tariq sat on his stool, took the pen and ink out, and started writing on a new white sheet of paper the next page of Surah Taha. His hands moved intently and carefully across the white sheet of paper laid in front of him on the stand. He worked tirelessly until 5 a.m. when he was almost done with the *surah*. He promised to continue at night after work and headed to the shower to get ready for *fajr salat* and work.

Chapter 6

Hajaratu

WHEN ALONE IN HER office, she listened to the Codex, while lounging on her comfortable throne-like chair. The chair, which was bigger than her, earned her the title of Queen Hajar.

When people complimented it, she always replied, "Bilqis, may God be pleased with her, throne of 240 feet wide by 200 feet tall was a throne. That made people wonder if Bilqis, may God be pleased with her, was a giant. *Allahu alim.* My Creator's Kursi is the ultimate. This is nothing but *alhamdullilah.* Regardless, I feel fabulous sitting in it."

Listening to the Quran always took her back to when she started decoding the letters one by one and ultimately found a *tajweed* teacher to help her read it as it was revealed. Being in the paper and pulp industry, she felt blessed that her Lord had bestowed the love of the greatest manuscript, of His speech upon her. For this reason, Hajaratu made an extra effort to hold to higher standards anything book-related. You could call her bookish.

Hajaratu had a practice of discussing books, relationships articles or blog posts with her employees to get a feel for their mental fabric. This helped her connect with her employees on a deeper level. However, sometimes, even a proper background check or even her conclusions were not enough to detect fraud or ill-intent. Some people just knew out to fly safely under the radar until they were caught red-handed in the basket. The idea came to her one day when she was listening to a podcast about an interesting boss who regularly organized a party for her employees. At that party, she would send her psychiatrist to mingle with the crowd. Then over the days that followed, many employees would be let go, some promoted, etc. She found the woman's method disturbing but took whatever she thought beneficial in the method and carried on.

***

Hajar woke up for *tahajjud* every day even when she was on her period. If she couldn't touch the *mushaf*, she simply read from her phone. Since, it was the month of Rajab, she went for

Surah 17, The Night Journey. She normally recited *surahs* that called out to her. Having already completed a *khitmah* of the Quran, *alhamdullilah* the call or the pull these *surahs* had on her came naturally.

In busy times, she spent about thirty minutes connecting to her Lord during the peace of the night. When she had more time, she awoke at 3 a.m. and didn't resume her *tilawa*t, *nafila salat*, and *dhikr* until two hours later. She loved the sweetness and intimacy of these peaceful nights.

Then, she rested for a bit or took a shower before the call for *fajr* came to resume her *sila* to her Lord. All while remaining mindful with silent supplications and statements of gratitude.

She said thanks for being alive at her age. She was also grateful to be single and free. Being a widow had been a blessing she couldn't ignore. Yes, it came with challenges and labels, but it was all other people's opinions. "Those usually belong to the toilet," her therapist mentioned once, and she couldn't agree more.

After *fajr salat*, Hajaratu sat until she could perform *ishraq salat*. It was a Saturday morning so she could take extra time worshipping. During the week, she was out the door soon after *fajr*.

Next, she looked at her agenda and started her morning routine with self-affirmations, *duas*, and her to-do list; editing being a major to-do on the list. While she had editors, she still edited some manuscripts and approved editorial blogs and articles for her companies so that she didn't lose her hand at the gift. Once done with her journal, she made herself breakfast and sat at her computer to edit manuscripts for her company Shajaratun Publishing, LLC; a subsidiary of her main company Shajaratun, Inc. The parent company dealt with the wholesaling of raw materials; the trees, the land on which the trees was sitting, the logs of wood, the pulp, etc. She wasn't filthy rich like Bilqis, may God be pleased with her, but she was self-sufficient in her own right. A thing she always gave thanks for.

All the stories of Sulayman عليه السلام, of Bilqis رضي الله عنها, of Khadijah رضي الله عنها and the Prophet ﷺ reminded her of was that Allah ﷻ was al-Wahhab and ar-Razzaq. And that He ﷻ was the Inheritor of all. *SubhanAllah.*

At about mid-day, she paused and ate a croissant, tomato basil soup and a homemade leafy lettuce salad layered with tomato, onion, salt, pepper, shredded white cheese, and olive oil.

After eating, she took a thirty-minute nap and then woke up for the next *salat, zhur.* She was very diligent about her *salat*, a bit too calculated.

Saturday afternoons were the time she used to go grocery shopping even if Salif, her chef, did most of the shopping. So, she set out for the next task. She stopped at the *halal* grocery store and got some meat and then she headed to the African grocery store to get some plantains, yams, *attiéké*, and other essential ingredients and spices.

The young cashier, Koffi, always asked her the same questions.

"Are you married?"

"No," she always replied.

"Can I see your hair?"

"Absolutely not!"

Then he would retell the same story of one his classmate in Ghana that his friends and he, as a joke, pulled the *hijab* off. He felt bad for it.

She wondered now if it was his curiosity that was getting the best of him. Since he couldn't act the way he did when he was foolish and young. Perhaps, he was looking for a polite way to satisfy his curiosity about the privacy of a woman he has no right seeing. She was always nice to him while shaking her head. Many times, his chat felt like advances, but she dismissed that impression.

After paying for her groceries, Koffi helped her put the purchases in her trunk and said goodbye.

Once at home, she replayed in her mind a call she had made to her niece Taherah.

"*Assalamu aleikum,* Auntie!"

"*Wa aleikum salam,* Taherah. What you up to on your day off?"

"You know, the usual stuff when I am not working for you or when you are not holding me hostage!" she playfully said.

Hajaratu gasped. "I see how it is. You are dead to me," she joked and made a clicking sound like hanging up with her mouth.

"I am kidding, you know I love you. You are the Best Aunt I know," Taherah cajoled her.

"I am your only aunt," Hajaratu taunted.

"Yes, but compared to all my uncles, you win."

"Now, she is comparing me to men! This is what I get from being single and a businesswoman."

"You are *so* dramatic!" Taherah said and cut their playful banter short by asking another question. "I'm preparing for Ramadan. I ordered decorations, some special *bakhour,* and I'm already working on *eid* gifts!"

"Oh, my goodness, I know the companions, may Allah ﷻ be pleased with them, prepared six months in advance but for some reasons I feel like you are over the top already."

"That's because you live every day like it is a day in Ramadan. I am so jealous," Taherah teased.

"Maybe." Hajaratu replied, shrugging her shoulders. She spread out her legs on the length of her nine-seater beige couch and turned on the huge flat screen TV. Adjusting the comfy living-room blanket on her legs, she zapped through the channels without settling on one.

"I wish you had found that guy that Allah ﷻ has created for you by this Ramadan." Taherah said, wishfully.

"I know. Ramadan nights would have been lit in another way, but if he is not going to treat me like the Prophet ﷺ treated his wives, especially his wife Khadijah, رضي الله عنها I am not interested."

"May Allah ﷻ grant us each of us that righteous spouse, *aameen!*

I certainly want the one to treat me the way the Prophet ﷺ treated Aisha رضي الله عنها."

"A*meen* to that Neecee! You are an Aisha for sure." And they laughed. When Hajaratu's words settled in, Taherah asked for more clarification.

"What do you mean I am an Aisha?" Taherah asked, genuinely.

"Remember when she was slandered?"

"Yes…" Taherah prodded her to continue.

"OK, the Prophet ﷺ interviewed her maid. This one said that aside from the fact that her mistress was not a good cook, she didn't see any issue with Aisha's رضي الله عنها character."

"Oh, I see. Thanks for the clarification."

"Anytime, Dear Neece."

Hajaratu smiled at the memory of that conversation. Another Ramadan was upon her, and she tried to find strength in patience and sought refuge from despair. So, she called her dear niece again. After their regular small talk, she said, "On another note, I would invite you to hang out with me but then you will be spending seven out of seven days with me. And it's not fair. You are much younger and need to be with people your age."

"Pfff, only fifteen-years. I am happy that after my internship you offered me a position. It's so flexible with a grown-up salary. Thank you. *Alhamdullilah*."

"It was your *rizq,* Habibti. Remember, if you find better, please don't be shy to tell me."

"It's not going to happen, but noted. Do you have *Thiep Djen* with fish in your fridge?"

"Yes, like I would run out of that ever. Ask a different question." Hajaratu added, laughing.

"I am coming over." Tahera announced. "See you in a bit." She abruptly hung up.

Hajaratu stared at her receiver, shook her head while smiling and tried to find a channel to focus on before the arrival of her ravenous niece who loved food but hated cooking.

Chapter 7

Hajaratu

TAHERAH ARRIVED IN A blur of Arabic greetings, French kisses, and shoved her head into her aunt's fridge. "Where is your cat?"

"She is outside as usual. I was petting her earlier. You know when it gets a bit warm, she can do without my affection. When it gets cold, she is right back on my lap and demands attention and gets mad if I don't want to mess with her for abandoning me during her good times outside, haha!"

"You and girlfriend cat have issues…" Taherah said, rolling her eyes. "Anyway, let me continue looking in your fridge. Oh! You ordered *Poulet Yassa*, too!"

"Yeah! You know I like to mix it up and keep it interesting. About the cat, heh, our love relationship is complicated. By the way, how do you fast during Ramadan?" Hajaratu asked her niece, baffled. "You eat like an ogre."

"Have you seen a real ogre before?" Taherah threw her head out of the fridge, squinting her eyes at her aunt. Then, her head disappeared back into the huge cooling box, scavenging for drinks and desserts.

"It's beside the point, and you get what I am trying to say," Hajaratu countered.

"It's a mind game. I mentally prepare myself for the month. I talk to myself, you know."

"That I already knew."

"When is your cleaning lady coming again?" Taherah asked.

"Are you trying to poach her again?"

"Of course! She is so sweet…"

Hajaratu just shook her head and rolled her eyes. Then she added, "Has my chef accepted to cook for you, too?"

"You know I can be convincing," she replied with a cheeky smile.

"How convincing?" her aunt teased, wiggling her eyebrows suggestively.

Taherah just giggled and soon they burst into another fit of laughers.

When they had calmed down, Taherah took the floor. "I am asking for my future husband to cook in my *nikah* contract, for sure!"

"Why not? Go you." Hajaratu encouraged. "Actually, it's not that farfetched. My friend's mom had a similar arrangement. They are South Asians. It was unheard of back then, but it worked for them. She took care of other tasks in their homes."

"See! I knew I wasn't too demanding." Taherah let out, yelping excitedly.

"Right, we the AbuBouakais, are never demanding," Hajaratu said sarcastically.

"First of all, I prefer AbuBakr. African people are always twisting Arabic names anyway they see fit." Taherah pointed out. "Second of all, I have superior taste." And she threw her head in the air mock-imperiously.

"Oh, dear niece, you are too entertaining for your own good," Hajaratu said, laughing.

"Thank you. Thank you." Tahera finished while bowing her head to an invisible audience for the performance she just put on.

"Besides, take the streets of Istanbul or India, men rule the street food's business with their large pots of foods or elegant restaurants. Women chefs are trying to get recognized by fighting for the title of chef all the over the world."

"Right. I am happy with my job," Taherah simply agreed.

***

It had a been six weeks since Hajaratu had returned from Indonesia and resumed work. This week, she had meetings with her sellers, and they updated her on what progress they had made while she was out.

"Cypress, how did the meeting with Waraqa Tissue, Inc. go?"

"They liked our raw materials and put in some orders, so we have secured that account."

"Good job Cypress, *alhamdullilah*." Then, she turned her attention to Renée. "How did your pitch go with the carpenters for our imported logs of wood?"

"I gave them samples to try out and proposed them a lower quote. Yesterday, they confirmed to me that we won the bid."

"Excellent!" Hajaratu praised. Then she went around the table and talked to each of her employees until she got to the last.

"Angelique, how did it go with your assigned potential vendor; The Stationary Kings?"

Angelique disdainfully gave her attention to her red manicured nails and then she replied, "It went fine. I didn't get the gig." She pursed her lips.

"Really?" Hajaratu asked.

"Yes, they were not interested in your products," Angelique said and shrugged her shoulders. Insolence radiated from her pores. The room was dead quiet.

"I heard a different story," Hajaratu advanced carefully.

"Which is?"

"My reliable sources told me that that you presented a competitor's product to them. Is that true?"

"Yes, it's true."

"You signed a non-competition agreement," Hajaratu reminded her.

"Correct. My resignation letter will be on your desk tomorrow," she panned and strolled out of the room with her head held high.

A couple years before that, Hajaratu would have been hot. She would have fired Angelique and made a scene. Had she not taken a class on purification of the heart; it would have become very ugly on the spot. She had learned to be remain dignified, like the Prophet ﷺ when people acted a fool with her.

"I look forward to it," is all she said and turned her attention to the rest of her employees. "The door is wide open for anyone else who wants to leave. When no one moved, she said, "Thank you for your hard work. The meeting is adjourned."

"Taherah, please stay. I need to talk to you."

Taherah sat back down and reopened her agenda, waiting for the conference room to empty.

"Did you know that she was selling her own products?"

"I had no idea," Taherah replied. "Dang. You have people everywhere!"

"I do. I have to protect my interests. I am not forcing anyone to be here. We all have a prescribed *rizq,* so I won't sweat anything not decreed for me. She can go wherever she pleases. Please make sure her letter is on my desk tomorrow morning. This is the fifth person who deceives me, and I didn't want the situation to get heated and physical like it did a couple times. We had to call security."

Taherah sighed and then continued speaking, "Will do. Do you want me to tell HR?"

"Yes, please inform HR to remove her from the system today. I don't need her coming back here tonight and messing around with my files and contacts. Make sure her keycard is inactive today."

"Yes, Ma'am."

"Should we start recruiting another person?" Taherah asked.

"Yes, you know the drill. Please share the link with me when the job is posted. I have someone qualified in mind."

"This is new. I usually know all your beeswax. Care to expound?" Taherah asked, curiously.

"It's a A and B's affair. C yourself out."

"Salty! Especially, since that trip in Indonesia."

"Yes, I am," Hajaratu replied, grumbling. She didn't tell her about that trip, but it was all that played in her mind. Young and old men giving her proposals, none of which she could assess the real motives. So, she closed all the doors to protect her heart and her business. "Ya Allah guide me," she whispered.

***

Later that night after she arrived home, Taherah emailed Hajaratu the link to the new position that opened up at her company. When her phone pinged to notify her, "*Alhamdullilah,*" she said in a low voice. She had been patiently waiting for the green light. Hajaratu finally got an excuse to call Tariq. She had stared at his business card so many times wanting to call him because her ears craved his sweet compliments even though part of her reprimanded her for such scandalous desires.

She called him, but he didn't pick-up. So, she left him a voicemail asking him to call her back.

"*Salams,* it's Hajaratu with the interesting name. We met at the symposium in Indonesia. I have a new position that just opened up at Shajaratun, Inc. So, I wanted to see if you would be interested in a new challenge. *Masalam*."

She exhaled deeply afterwards and crashed onto her living room couch, burying her head deeply in the cushions. She was collapsing after all the courage she had to muster to do this complicated thing with mixed intentions.

She could still imagine his fit arms and chest through his long sleeve shirt when he had removed the jacket to drape it around her shoulders. She still had the suit jacket. She had forgotten to return it, and he had never asked. From time to time, she would smell it while closing her eyes. This is the closest she got to any intimacy. Her *taqwa* had rightfully prevented her from transgressing. And it was a *jihad* alright.

Chapter 8

Tariq

SHE ACTUALLY CALLED ME. Tariq kept repeating to himself. He was bewildered.

He remembered his talk with uncle when he returned to the states like it was yesterday. It had been about a month and a half since.

"*Assalamu aleikum,* Tonton," Tariq said into the phone with a deep and leveled voice.

"*Wa aleikum salam,* son! How was your trip?"

"It was productive. I made new connections; business and otherwise..." Tariq cleared his throat quickly.

"Hmm, otherwise? What does that mean, Tariq?"

"I met a woman I really liked while doing business. But she seems a bit older. Is that even wise for me to pursue her?"

"It depends." His uncle added after a short pause.

"Is she a '*Innaha kanat, wa kanat*' or a Mrs. Robinson type of woman?"

"Hahahahahah!" Tariq laughed and chuckled for a while until he could find his voice.

"Uncle, I can always count on you to bring me an expression I am not expecting! A *seerah*'s quote?"

"Is she like the Prophet ﷺ described Khadijah رضي الله عنها to Aisha رضي الله عنها meaning does she have class, status, intellect, etc. Or does she give you a predator vibe that your *nafs* enjoys a bit? Am I right or am I right?"

"Well, she was reserved. I actually preyed on her because I felt a pull toward her when she entered the room. Unfortunately, I didn't get a chance to interact a lot with her. Our conversation was cut off short and I gave her my card."

"Well, make *dua* and perform *istikhara* for Allah ﷻ to guide you insha'Allah. Allah is al-Mubeen; we will know what course of action to take soon insha'Allah."

Tariq talked to his uncle about other details of his trip, asked about his aunt and then hung up feeling a little guided. "Ya Allah if she is for me, let her seek me out, *aameen*."

Fast forward six-weeks later, there was a sign of life from her. *She is not technically seeking me out in the way I intended, but it's a step closer toward the right direction.*

He made a quick *dua* and then called his uncle Faliku for insight.

"*Assalamu aleikum,* Tonton."

"*Wa aleikum salam,* son! What's new?"

"She called."

"And?"

"She said she has a position open at her company, and she would like me to apply for it. I have not returned her call yet."

"Good. By the way, give me her name so I can Google her. I was actually talking about your predicament to your aunt, and she asked me if I did some research on this woman and I couldn't answer her."

"You people are nosey, but I did walk right into that."

Tariq gave him Hajaratu's name, and his uncle instructed him to give him a minute.

"Let me go into my study so I can look her up on my computer."

"Sure," Tariq replied, imagining his uncle bringing about him the wide sides of his favorite embroidered African kaftans—*bubu bazin*— that he loves to wear at home, then getting up and adjusting his thin reading spectacles on his nose in order to see or go perform a task, and dragging his feet in his house slippers, like Tariq has seen him do countless times.

"Tariq, are you still there?"

"Yes, Tonton."

"I thought your phone went dead for a second. Anyway, I found her. She is not bad-looking. She has class and is wealthy. She can use your flair in her business. I am not saying that she is not good at her thing, but she could use your outlets and unique touch—"

"What picture of her did you come across?" asked Tariq.

"The one with the elegant baby blue abaya with the pearly lace dentelle on the sleeves."

"I like that picture," Tariq let out, forgetting to control himself.

"Lower your gaze, son! She will be your boss insha'Allah."

"In another era, I could have married her. Today, I would never see the end of sexual harassments claims."

"True. Now that she is offering you a job, are you sure you want to apply? This can turn into a *fitnah* for you." His uncle pointed out with a serious tone.

Before he could answer, his aunt snatched the phone from his uncle and asked, "Wanting an older woman is no easy task, son. Take some time to decide. We will be here."

"Good night, auntie," he said, wondering when she arrived at his uncle's side in the study or if she was a third listener in the private conversation all along. He chuckled to himself and said goodbye and then hung up.

***

Tariq applied and was selected for an interview. First with HR and then another one with Hajaratu and her team.

After the call, Hajaratu asked the team what they thought.

"We are short on staff, but he was good," Mahogany said.

"He is fine. I like him but I was hoping we would be hiring another girl," Cypress said.

Both had been hired because they were able to outshine their co-applicants, and because of their unique names, and their unusual expertise in the realm of trees. So, Hajaratu valued their opinions.

"Let's do this. We will hire him, and the girl and they will be both on probation until after six months. The best of the two will be officially hired," she finished.

"I think that is a great idea," Taherah chimed in.

"Taherah, please have IT send both candidates the background check authorization forms. After that, we will give them an offer."

***

"There is another issue that is bothering me a bit," Tariq said in a call shortly after accepting the offer from HR.

"OK…What is it?" Hajaratu asked, hesitantly.

"I don't plan to move to your city. I plan on travelling home once a month on the weekends to take care of my small business down here and see my family. Of course, I won't be competing with your company in your outlets."

"That's fine and your tact is much appreciated. The company can cover your travel expenses, but you are welcome to stay in one of my pool houses if that's cheaper for you. I have a chef and a housekeeper on call. They will cater to your needs, if you choose. My assistant uses them at will." She laughed.

"Let me think about it," he replied, smiling.

"Of course," she added.

"Which mosque is closest to there?"

"Just Google it. There is one seven minutes from here, but I like to go to Carrollton. It's like 15 to 20 mins with the tollway," she said.

"Okay, thanks."

***

Tariq's uncle dropped him at the airport and gave him plenty of advice about going to live with a woman, especially one he had a soft spot for.

"Be careful. I don't need to remind you that every time you feel that pull and the whispers because you are alone with her, you need to seek protection with Allah and leave the room immediately. And the best of provision is *taqwa*."

"Yes, Tonton."

"Older women need some lovers," his aunt pointed out. She was ambivalent on the subject since she had many friends in the situation of his future boss; single older attractive women with no attractive prospective. Yes, their biological clocks were ticking but that didn't mean they shouldn't be happy with a young man if they chose to. They had had plenty of discussions on how this could work in present days but came away empty handed from their speculations. Finally, they all settled on, "Make *dua* and let Allah ﷻ decree the rest."

So, Tariq did his best not to stress over the future.

He arrived at Dallas Love Field Airport and Hajaratu's chauffeur picked him up. He chatted a bit with the driver until they arrived to her home in Northpark, closer to downtown. If he had any doubt that she was loaded, he no longer had those doubts. She lived in an affluent neighborhood. Her mansion was two stories and sprawling.

Once past the gate, the staff welcomed him and showed him his quarters. He called Hajaratu to let her know that he had arrived as she was working late in the office.

"Welcome to Dallas! Freshen up and eat. There is plenty of food. Get plenty of rest, too. We have a lot of work to do tomorrow."

"Thank you! No problem, will do. If I don't see you tonight, I guess it will be at the office indeed insha'Allah."

"Right. We can ride together but you can make other arrangements if you want to leave early or late."

"Thank you for being so generous," he added.

"You are my guest and my employee now. So, *alhamdullilah* for everything."

Tariq slept early that night. The next day, he hit the ground running by introducing her to new outlets. With Hajaratu, he was different. He asserted himself and flirted with her anytime they were alone.

"I could be your mom or your older sister," she told him once, giggling.

Once Taherah told her, after observing the duo for a moment without them knowing, "Auntie, your new employee is actually fine… And he only has eyes for you. Y'all so cheesy with the niceties you say to each other when you think no one sees you. Do you like him?"

"I do but I am too old for him. I know I shouldn't flirt back when he does but I can't stop myself."

"Well, if you want to pursue it, we can find a way to make it *halal*. You are on a clock!" she said, while pointing at her wrist. And she would dutifully continue to point at her wrist every time she caught them lightly flirting because she was the secretary. They would normally knock it off the minute a third person arrived.

Chapter 9

Hajaratu

MONTH AFTER MONTH, TARIQ and Hajaratu fell into a comfortable routine. He went home once a month to see his relatives and tend to his business needs, then he returned on Monday morning and went straight to work. At night, he stayed in his corner of her mansion unless he needed food or something from the main house. He always gave her plenty of warning before approaching her private area and she appreciated his mindfulness.

Before Ramadan, Salif approached Hajaratu for the meal plan she had in mind for the holy month.

"Hi, Salif. How are you?"

"I am good. Thank you, Madame."

"Good. So, just make salads daily, a millet porridge, and a variety of sandwiches. I will have the sandwiches for *suhur*. I also want some rice, a stew of your liking, and a vegetable dish every other day or simply cook one big pot once a week. I will get the fruits. Finally, one healthy dessert will be nice. We can eat it slowly since Tariq and Taherah eat here on the regular."

"You got it, Ms. Hajaratu," he said, smiling. She wondered if he was smiling at the mention of Tariq or the Convincing Taherah. She eyed him a bit, but she couldn't read him, so she let it go. He was always formal with her, and he also dressed formally with his impeccable chef clothes. She found him on Instagram one day as she was scrolling aimlessly in her down time. She liked the fact that he was from West Africa and was familiar with the food in her country. A Malian, he was born in the US. His family, contrary to the norm, supported his calling and today he made a decent living catering to various events and households.

She added, "Before I forget, I want to invite some of my friends with their husbands mid-Ramadan for *iftar*.

"What do you want on the menu for that day?" Salif asked while taking notes.

"Hmm, I have some African American friends in the group so please make a casserole of mac and cheese. Then some fried plantains. Please make sure that the plantains are ripe and just right. I want the real *alloco* not chips." She laughed at herself.

59

"Okay." Salif said, nodding and still writing in the guest chair facing her desk in her home study.

"Please make a chocolate cake, some jollof rice, a Caesar salad for sure, some *gboflotos*—Ivorian donuts. They really like these donuts. Please make a fruit salad with mangoes, some ginger juice, some *bissap*, and some tamarind juice."

"Do you want some orange juice or lemonade, too?"

"Sure. Please make some baobab juice, too."

"Noted."

"Did we cover everything?"

"We have not talked about appetizers. I have something in mind," Salif said. "How about some white bean fritters and a spicy sauce like the Burkinabe side dish.

"Hmm, please make them. I grew up eating them actually. OK, if we miss anything we will assess the situation a couple days before and cross that bridge then insha'Allah."

"That sounds good."

"Thank you, Salif."

"You are welcome, Madame."

When Ramadan arrived, Malik, the chauffeur, drove Hajaratu and Tariq to *taraweeh* daily. The drive to and from the mosque was usually quiet while a Quranic lecture played in the background. For *fajr,* Tariq always offered to lead the *salat.* He told her once, "I would be a useless body if I didn't lead the prayer in this welcoming home from time to time."

Hajaratu secretly enjoyed these *salat* bonding times. She also enjoyed listening to his strong voice from the pool room when he was up late at night reciting the Codex or when he recited in the empty *masjid* when they arrived too early for communal *salat,* as the Islamic school students were still finishing up their *iftars* or *suhur.* She quietly did the same after greeting the *masjid* with two *rakats* reminding herself to compete in good for the sake of Allah ﷻ. She would grab a neat Quran from the shelves and read the coded letters and let their meaning sink into her heart.

Midway through the prayer, which took close to two hours, because after the seventeen rakats there was usually a short *khaterah* about a theme in the Quran, they made their way out to meet up with the chauffeur. Sometimes before leaving she would catch up with some of the students who were her friends, like Fateenah and Zêguêla, or other members of the community like Qari, Sana, and Anika who used the same *masjid* as her.

The first week of Ramadan, it was uneventful in the car, like their daily commute to work. She normally worked on her tablet while he sat there answering or replying to emails on his smartphone or Macbook.

The second week started, and during one ride Tariq cleared his throat on the way back to her house from the *masjid*.

Chapter 10

Tariq

"REMEMBER THAT LAST DAY in Indonesia?" he asked hesitantly.

"Oh yeah, you said it felt like Ramadan. It was a lovely night." She noted, calmly.

"We had a great time for sure," he said, smiling. "I miss those types of conversations. Every day, we enter the car, and we act like complete strangers when we both know that we had a connection once; a spark that I want to ignite again." He confessed, exhaling, and inhaling her soft perfume. Being in her proximity had been a sweet torture. The level of self-control he had to muster not to sit closer to her and smell her all night was weighing on him. Visions of kissing her had even crossed his mind. Her full lips teased him every time she smiled at him to compliment him on his work or to greet him. What is a man to do when he is attracted to his boss who is also his landlady?

Suddenly a wild curiosity overtook him, and he let himself go impulsively.

"What is the name of your perfume?"

"It's not a perfume. It's a blend of oil I use on my skin; the main ingredients are olive oil, black seed oil, and frankincense oil. Hopefully, I won't be considered an adulteress since you can smell it. I tried to decrease the use so it's not overpowering but it's hard to calibrate sometimes."

"Wow, you think of everything. In any case, it smells nice. I wish we can connect more like that night in Indonesia where we were freer."

"Don't forget that we weren't alone that day as He was watching us and we are not alone today, either. We have at least two witnesses."

"More reasons to talk since we have chaperones." he said with a spreading smile.

She laughed at his dangerous game.

"Plus, you work too much. You need to relax a bit."

She sighed. "I pour the energy I have for a companion into my work. I have to keep myself occupied so I don't transgress," she said and lowered her head embarrassingly.

"I run to get it out of my system," he said.

"I have a treadmill, but I need foodgasms," she dropped naughtily.

"For real?!" he said, amazed.

"See what you made me say after *taraweeh*. *Astaghfirullah!*" Then she kept quiet.

"Let's play a game when we return. I promise to leave the minute it gets awkward. I also promise not to intrude."

"It's late. Plus, I don't usually talk like that in front of my driver. He respects me, you know," Hajaratu said, side-eying Tariq with pouting lips.

"He knows you have needs. We all do. Come on, it's harmless." A tense moment passed before her jubilant reply.

"Fine! Now I am curious, and it will drive me crazy if I refuse a little opportunity to relax."

***

When they arrived home, he told her that the kitchen was where he wanted to play.

"Okay…" she said, intrigued.

"Please sit at one of the stools while I look in the fridge. He quickly peeked in the fridge and exclaimed, "Perfect."

Then he said, "Permission to approach you from the back? I won't touch you. I just need to veil your eyes."

"Hmm, okay…"

Tariq went behind Hajaratu and stood there a minute letting out a slow warm breath. He could tell the heat of his hot breath on her back sent a shiver to her body. She balled her fists and released them and trembled a bit. He removed his dusty pink tie from his pocket, delicately tied it around her eyes, and asked, "Is it too tight?"

"No, it's perfect."

"Can you see?" he asked.

"No."

"Good. Welcome to Tariq's food testing game! I'm single so I know how to cook for myself, even though I really do appreciate your chef."

"What?! Really? Pff. I am still full from *iftar*." She exclaimed. She knew she shouldn't eat more and feed her *nafs* but, she couldn't stop herself from declining his offer.

"You are hungry, and I will prove it. A different type of hungry."

Tariq quickly grabbed a few things from the fridge, and she heard the stove's flame screech a few times, then the microwave was put to use, and a few minutes later, he approached her. The smell of various enticing flavors; chocolate, fruits, vanilla... distracted her for a moment, exiting her lower self.

"I am done. That was not too bad right?" Tariq said, now about 15 minutes into this secret cooking game.

"If you say so. Anyway, hurry up, we have work tomorrow."

"Yes, Madame." he added, jokingly.

He gently fed her the first bite on a fork and asked her to tell him what she thought she was eating.

"A chocolate pancake, hmm…it's so soft and rich…" she involuntarily moaned deeply as he slowly removed the fork between her lips.

He cleared his throat and said, "It's a crêpe."

"Same difference," she argued.

"Pancakes are too heavy, crêpes are lighter. Anyway, next up! Another dessert. Tell me what you think it is." He carefully inserted the fork into her mouth, enjoying the sensuality of the moment.

"It is my strawberry pie!" she retorted, knowingly. Then, she let the richness of the dessert coat her tongue while experiencing the sweetness in all her senses. She grunted and choked back another moan.

"It's a five-minute strawberry cheesecake," he said, breathing hoarsely.

"No way…" she said, her voice hoarse.

Chapter 11

Hajaratu

SHE DIDN'T WANT TARIQ's fork to leave her mouth the second time. Or any other time. He fed her seemingly simple little things that somehow blew her mind and made her tastebuds explode. He struggled with her tight full lips around the metal before she let go every time. Finally, she grabbed his tie off her face and threw it on the floor, staring at him in a panicked-like mode. He was wild-eyed and chest-heaving, enjoying the show. She didn't dare look down toward the lower part of his body. The upper part of his body had already betrayed him.

Afraid to transgress any further, she ran to her room and bolted the door before sliding down to the floor to resume her heavy breathing. She was hot and bothered. She quickly went through her night routine, dropping nearly everything she touched out of her shaking hands before finally getting into bed while uttering a protection *dua*. She was completely uncentered.

The next day, Hajaratu asked the housekeeper, Korotum, to stop by.

"Please burn some sage and then some *usunan—bakhour* in the house today." She omitted telling her that she wanted Shaytan to leave her palace.

"OK, Tantie," Korotum said.

"Do you have a busy schedule today?" Hajaratu asked.

"Not really. I only have to see a few clients and then stop by your niece's place."

"I see. No problem. You take care. Bye."

"Bye, Tantie," she said.

Korotum had a hard time discarding the title of respect she used for her employer even after Hajaratu repeatedly told her she could call her "Grande Soeur," meaning Big Sister, since they were kin.

Chapter 12

☪

Tariq

The day before--after the food tasting

TARIQ QUICKLY CLEANED THE kitchen and left the main house. Back in his room, he replayed in his mind each of her expressions every time he fed her. *She was such a good eater and pleasing to look at.* He could imagine her tongue swirl around the fork inside her mouth. And the thought almost made him release in his pants. He had no idea where the thought of cooking for her had entered his mind. *My nafs. Right…*

He had not lowered his gaze. On top of that, her soft moans drove him insane. He was positive that if he didn't clean his heart before sleeping, he would have a wet dream, and she would be at the root of it.

The way she wriggled on that chair made him picture things his mind should not even wander to. But it was too late, and he couldn't unsee his mind's creations any longer. *Now, I will have to lower my gaze because I can't look at her anymore. These images will always show up!* He mentally chastised himself, even though he thoroughly enjoyed the heat and intimacy of the moment. They had played with fire and were very close to a burn. *Astagfirullah*. He quickly repented but didn't expound on his *tazkiyah* and fell off the wagon with the troubled night he experienced.

The next day, he took an Uber to work, still reeling from the naughty dreams he had. When Hajaratu arrived at work, she greeted her team normally and then buried herself in her office.

Tariq planned to avoid her for the rest of week. He was embarrassed and still hot at the sight of her. He was having issues cooling down within her mere proximity.

The end of the week arrived, and he debated if he should attend the *iftar* dinner in the main house, which she had previously invited him to. He normally travelled back home at this time of month, but he already canceled his travel plans that week. Now he wished he had not canceled his trip back home. Since he didn't want to spend the night alone, he decided to go to the dinner when the other invited men arrived with their wives. Hajaratu had told Tariq that she had invited a few of her non-Muslim white neighbors, and that there would be at least five couples, and several single women and men. He planned to revolve around the men. Salif and Malik would be attending along with the niece of his landlady. She was a girl with whom he shared a name. Taherah resembled Hajaratu a bit, but he preferred the latter's beauty and the spark he felt when she was around. Taherah had interacted with him at work and a couple times in the main house. She was always to the point and respectful.

"Hey, *salams,* homonym, the boss needs you." Or "Hey, *salams,* homo. HR still needs a signature from you about a deposition..." Even with the odd way of teasing him, she was always concise and breezy.

The first time she called him homo with the first "o" pronounced short instead of long, he whipped his head around and asked himself, "What did she call me?"

After seeing his surprise, she explained that they had the same name. Homonyms. He laughed, and they kept a superficial amical bond since. Above all, he respected her.

Chapter 13

☪

The Katib

RAMADAN THAT YEAR FELL during the spring, so the guests started to arrive after 7:30 p.m. The couples, which included Femta Traoré and Uthman Syed, Qari Fofana and Abdul Malik Jefferson, Zêguêla Raghad Karamoko and Zayd Abbas, Fateenah Lewis and Marc Lewis, Dawn Cooper and Miles Brown, all arrived amazingly on time along with the single guests. Her South Asian friend Sana was amongst the singles, along with Taherah and some of Taherah's Muslim friends; a man and woman from college.

When the *adhan* for *iftar* rang from the various Muslim guests' prayer apps, Salif promptly passed bowls of dates to the men and another bowl to the women. Taherah helped him cater to the women so they could be efficient. The rest of the food was spread across the dinner table ready for them to eat after *salah*.

Malik, the chauffeur, led the *salah* after Tariq called the *iqamat*. After the *maghrib* prayer, Hajaratu gave a quick speech. "*Assalamu* aleikum everyone! Good evening. Thank you for accepting our invitation to break the fast with us. Food is ready, so eat as much as you want, and may God bless us all, *aameen*."

A lot of *aameen* echoed back and the women queued first to serve themselves. They congregated on one side of the room with their plates in their hands. Then the men did the same. Tariq caught the eye of Hajaratu a few times but couldn't hold her gaze long. He quickly looked away and tried to distract himself by getting to know all the men in the room.

He learned that Miles was the neighbor, Uthman was from Somalia, that Abdul Malik and Marc were African Americans, and that finally Zayd was Sudanese and a student of knowledge. They all did various things for work from accounting to IT.

Tariq complemented Zayd's lush but neat beard.

"Thanks man! You will fit right into our bromance," Zayd chuckled and continued, "That black seed oil does some wonders guys!"

"We see," all the men said in unison. So Zayd added, "Ya Allah give us your love, the love of the people you love and the love of the actions that will bring us closer to you, *aameen!*"

All the Muslim men said *aameen* while Miles remained stunned and intrigued by them. He began firing off questions which they tried to answer to the best of their abilities. At one point he asked, "So, what kind of changes you have to make to your life during Ramadan besides not eating from daybreak to sunset?"

"A lot and not a lot. I see it as an oxymoron. One, we are supposed to already do that daily, but at the same time, many of us for Ramadan get into a boot camp kind of mode to control our carnal desires. We strive for blessings, God mindfulness, charity work, and most of all to have good character," Zayd answered.

"Why good character?" Miles asked.

"Have you ever been hungry and more quickly lost your temper?"

"Actually, that makes sense now," Miles conceded. "So, how about, uh, intimacy? How do you deal with no…you know, with your wives for a whole month?"

The Muslim men all laughed, and the singles smiled cheekily.

"Who told you about *that?* We can have relations, but only between sunset to daybreak," Zayd replied again.

"Oh, during the opposite time of fasting, you are free to do anything permitted? Or *halal* like you put it."

"Exactly," the group of Muslim men acquiesced in unison. The men continued their discussions on one side of the room, sitting on or standing near the long beige sofa. They were oblivious of the women's conversations a few feet away from them. The joyous gathering was surrounded by beautiful Islamic Tableaux on the white walls.

***

On the women's side, sitting on another spacious nine-seater sofa, after the close friends caught up on each other's lives they started grilling Hajaratu. "Who was the *muezzin* with the voice similar to Imam Sudais?" Sana asked inquisitively. "He is cute, masha'Allah!"

"Oh, he is one my new sales representatives. He is from out of town, Minnesota to be precise, so he stays in the pool house for now."

"What?!" they all exclaimed.

"You are causing yourself some *fitnah,* my dear," Raghad pointed out, tssking disapprovingly, but still laughing.

Oh, Hajaratu already knew all about that *fitnah* they were referring to. Just last week, she had walked right into it and yet, the object of that *fitnah* was still in her lair.

"She is right, you are courting trouble. Just don't sleep-walk to his room one night. Haha!" Femta let out, and they all busted out laughing.

Then Fateenah chimed in. "How do you feel about him?" she asked, winking.

Hajaratu remained quiet, dropping her head and stifling a laugh.

"Oooss…," they all said on cue.

"That bad!?" Fateenah chuckled.

"He is so young!" Hajaratu said with a hint of disappointment.

"So?!" They all said in unison.

"And I am his boss."

"Well, Rasul ﷺ worked for Kadijah رضي الله عنها al-Kubrah!"

"True…however, today I can get sued for that."

They all sighed at that reality.

"Enough about me. How about you and your Ramadan nights? How are you dealing with romance on top of everything else?" Hajaratu inquired.

"Usually, it's easy to have some type of romance when I don't have to cook on days like today because usually the party or celebrating atmosphere follows us home and one thing leads to another..." Qari said, shrugging.

The women agreed and continued to share their non-incriminating tips with each other.

"If you are single, get a cat!" Fateenah teased the singles in the group, like Sana and Aisha.

"Y'all make *duas* for us," Aisha requested.

"What is *dua*?" Dawn asked and they explained like they normally did with any unfamiliar word they thought she didn't understand. She had gotten good at picking up on Arabic words since she was often invited to their more formal women's events as well as girls' night-in get togethers.

"Who wants to bet that they will integrate your boy toy into their bromance?" Raghad asked, amusingly. All the women raised their hands and Hajaratu shook her head in mock disbelief. She had gasped at the term "boy toy" but it was useless, the women were cackling and making fun of her.

Before the night ended at Hajaratu's, Malik led the prayer again for *taraweeh* since it was too late to catch the first or even second set of *taraweeh* cycles at any *masjid*.

"Thank you all for coming. See you at *eid,* insha'Allah, for an encore on my end!" Hajaratu had told all her guests on their way out, sending them off with to-go boxes of leftover food. Over the coming weekends, the other women would also host *iftar* dinners and invite each other.

Chapter 14

☪

Tariq

WHEN TARIQ ARRIVED TO work alone the next week, Emmanuel aka Manu had accosted him.

"Must be nice to ride to work every day with the boss. But wait, today you are alone…" he tssked and then added, "Trouble in paradise?"

"Leave me alone man," Tariq replied, irritation thick and noticeable in his reply.

"I am just saying. We are not blind over here," Manu added, tauntingly.

"She was just doing me a favor because I am from out of town."

"Exactly my point. She makes you a lot of favors."

Manu continued expounding on the special treatments, but Tariq stopped engaging with him. He just took a long sigh and put on his headphones to start calling prospective clients and old clients.

Shortly afterwards, Hajaratu came in and Manu was still on the issue.

"Behold! The Queen has arrived. Make way. Welcome, Madame, we missed you."

"Good morning, Manu. How are you?"

"I am excellent now," he replied, smiling wide. "I am happy to know that I am not invisible to you.

"Get to work, Manu. I don't pay you to shirk around."

"My apologies, Madame. I was just concerned since your new pet arrived without you. So, I thought you were sick or something," he finished, with a tone that truly lacked deep concern.

"Manu, please don't pry in my personal life. There is a time for it. Now is not the time," on that note, Hajaratu went straight to her office. The rest of the team whistled and made exclamations, enjoying the obvious diss. But Manu wasn't done. He went to sit at his cubicle begrudgingly plotting his next move.

***

Another week started, *eid* was around the corner, and Tariq arrived at work alone and was left alone.

"Man, what happened between you guys? Did she hit on you or did you hit on her?" Manu continued with his inquisition.

"I have a lot of work to do. Thanks for your *concern*." Tariq finished, emphasizing "concern" by making air quotes with his hands.

Manu feigned shock and put his right hand to his chest. "That's cold man!"

"Should we talk to HR?" Tariq asked.

"Actually, maybe we should. I have a few things to report myself."

"Whatever man," Tariq said and went back to his seat, holding his mug of coffee he had just brewed in the staff kitchen. He was known to be chill, a drama-free person with positive and calm vibes. So, he wasn't going to start sliding now. The day nearly ended before he was called into Hajaratu's office.

"I will be right there," he said, hanging up the work phone. As he walked, Tariq saw people throughout the office exchanging knowing looks to communicate that he was in trouble. Tariq just made Musa's *aleihi salam dua* again to diminish his dread. So far, the *dua* always helped him in sticky situations, and he hoped that His Creator didn't forsake him in this moment, too. He looked at Manu's cubicle and noticed an empty chair. That gave him some relief. Even though Hajaratu's office had glass doors, so everyone could see the activity within at all times, Tariq knew Manu could create a twisted scenario in his mind based on just a little truth. Immediately, Tariq sought protection with Allah ﷻ from Shaytan and the whispers he cast in the hearts of people around him and inside his own heart.

He knocked at Hajaratu's sliding glass door, and she motioned him to enter.

"Have a seat," she told him.

"Thanks."

Chapter 15

Hajaratu

"ARE WE GOOD?" SHE asked, keeping her voice low and knowing full-well that this was wrong place to discuss their conundrum. But she had no choice, she barely saw him at home as he came late and left very early. She wasn't going to try to interact with him at hours that were dangerous to do so for her own honor, character, and chastity.

"I don't know," he replied. "Are we?"

"It has become awkward between us," Hajaratu said, exhaling while pushing a stack of papers away from her. She had made space in front of her on the glass-covered wooden desk to intertwine and rest her delicate and manicured hands. Her desk was large with an inbox at one corner and a laptop at the other. Waiting for his reply, she lounged comfortably in her throne.

Tariq lowered his head, and added with a heavy sigh, "I am sorry for pushing the envelope too far. I am not usually like this with women. It's simply different with you."

"I am sorry, too for listening to my *nafsul ammarah*. Now, we are in the *nafsul lawwamah* stage. May God forgive us, *aameen*. But we are sinners, let's try to act better in each other's presence and try to encourage each other away from transgression."

"I agree. How did you sleep that night?" he asked.

"I was perturbed all night. I had to make *ghusl* before cooling down. We are adults so let's talk like adults."

He laughed and added, "I like that."

"How did you sleep that night?" she returned his question back to him.

"It depends. My intention was to make *tawbah* before sleeping so the sickness doesn't lead to a...urm... dream about you. Unfortunately, you know how living in the 'I wish' dimension makes you unproductive and stuck in Shaytan's world, right?"

She nodded to indicate that she understood. Then, he resumed his line of thinking.

"Okay, I was stuck in limbo. So, I forgot to clean my heart, and I slept without praying. So, I was tortured with my desires. Of course, you were in my dreams. Long story short, I had to make *ghusl* upon waking up. I was ashamed of myself. But He ﷺ is extensively Merciful. *Alhamdullilah*."

"*Alhamdullilah*," she said, not voicing her shock at his wild dreams. She had tried to respect his privacy even though he shared tidbits with her. She appreciated his maturity in owning up to his shit right then.

"Anyway, since we are fasting this month to control our desires, let's try not to make this kind of love... or lust in Ramadan."

"Right, it just burnt our good deeds, *astaghfirullah*."

"*Astagfirullah*," she repeated.

Then, she raised her voice and changed the line of questioning. She inquired about his work duties and progress with current and prospective buyers and suppliers.

"Good job," she praised, and he left her office with his head high.

***

Later that day, Hajaratu received news from HR and her lawyer that one of her employees filed a claim of employee harassment and nepotism.

"Allahu Akbar! Are you serious?!" she said aloud to herself when she received the call from her lawyer followed immediately by an email from the HR.

Without pause, she left her office to look for Emmanuel.

"The team said that he left for lunch, and they have not seen him since," Taherah relayed to Hajaratu who had tasked her to find the troublemaker.

She called Tariq back into her office. She knew that if that fool Manu was present, he would have made some snarky comment like, "Twice in a day in her office. Lucky you man!"

She wished someone loved him so he wouldn't be looking for attention from her or in her workplace. She just wasn't interested in his type or feeding his ego in any way. She also knew he was projecting his issues on Tariq, but things were in such a grey area that she didn't know that one day she would have to face a situation where business and pleasure merged without her original intent. She had a rule never to mix the two. Lately she had made many concessions because she liked Tariq a bit. Now, this lack of steadfastness was blowing up in her face. While it had worked for some people, like Rasul ﷺ and Khadijah رضي الله عنها, Hajaratu was afraid for herself and her business. Manu was asking for a huge settlement to keep quiet and not announce to the news that she was a corrupt leader. *HasbunAllah wa animal wakil.*

She prayed and added. *Wa Ala lahi fayatawakkali Muminun*. She always thought of the stories of the predecessors as a model of life for when we face similar situations to theirs-- the way they dealt with slander, love, hardship, etc. The taller the hardship, the higher Allah ﷻ elevated their statuses. She wondered how hard it must have been for Maryam عليه السلام to carry on with people assuming the worst of her, her family, her teacher, and so on when she did nothing wrong. She lauded the strength of the woman for carrying a baby for nine months alone and then finding strength and piggy backing on her former *tawwakul* (that had inspired Prophet Zachariah عليه السلام to make *dua* for a son) to go face the music knowing how the things were likely going to hit the fan upon her return.

The dung is about to hit the fan in my life, too. She pinned. Regardless, she continued to make *dua*.

Chapter 16

Tariq

"ARE YOU KIDDING ME? He is serious?"

"He is very serious. He wants to ruin my business by asking for these many millions and all the accounts you are working on. He said he is senior to you. He doesn't realize that you brought your big accounts to us."

"*La hawla wa la quwatta illa billah!* He is insane!"

"Calm down. We need to come up with a plan." She proposed with a calm air he didn't know she truly had.

"I can't work for you anymore." He pointed out.

"No, you can't do that. This is just a challenge."

"I recognize that. He is jealous. Maybe if I am no longer in the picture he will back off and become reasonable."

"I doubt it. We are passed child's play now. Anyway, I have tasked my lawyers and their detective teams to turn over every stone about his past and to leave nothing unchecked. Especially sealed files."

"I will keep you in my prayers, but I must stop working for you. It's for the best."

Before she could protest, he put his keycard on the table and got up. He let himself out. Soon he was quickly grabbing his things from his cube. His colleagues kept asking him what was up, but he just said, "it was nice while it lasted here. We will keep in touch. I will miss you. Bye guys." And he was out.

That night Hajaratu was besides herself. She tossed and turned all night. The next morning, she decided to work remotely.

She called Malik to let him know.

"*Assalamu aleikum,* Brother Malik."

"*Wa aleikum salam,* Sister. Is there anything wrong?"

"I am a little under the weather today, so I won't be going to the office for a couple days. You can take the week off. I will pray *taraweeh* at home this week, insha'Allah."

"May Allah grant you *afya, aameen.*"

"*Aameen.* Thank you, Brother Malik. Have a good day. *Masalam.*"

"*Jazakh'Allah khair, masalam.*"

"*Wa iyyak,*" she replied, and then hung up. Brother Malik, who was also kin to her, had moved from New York to work with her. When he was back home, he used to drive politicians and public officials to their workplaces and events. When the civil war and several *coup d'états* erupted in Ivory Coast, he promptly left the county to find asylum in America, like many of their compatriots.

Around mid-day, she called Taherah while petting her black cat. She had purposely gone out to find him that morning for some company.

"I miss him Taherah," Hajaratu lamented to her niece over the phone after he had returned to his state. "We spent so much time together that he had become some kind of work husband. I love his demeanor, his jokes, his honesty, his careful and caring nature, and the list goes on. I am sprung! We have such deep conversations and I absolutely love it!"

"Aw! Auntie…How can I help you?"

"Just listen to me vent. He is in my system, and I don't how to remove him. I get many proposals I am indifferent to because I always find something preventing me to accept. But Tariq is the whole package I have been looking for."

Chapter 17

The Katib

OVER THE COURSE OF the next two weeks, the atmosphere at Shajaratun, Inc. was tense. All employees were stressed out about losing their jobs as Manu's impending lawsuit threatened to bankrupt the company and leave them all on the street.

Tariq's peaceful aura had added to the calm of the place. Now that he was also no longer around, that calm as well as his flair for business and great ideas, were noticeably missed.

"Auntie!" Taherah shrieked over the phone one of those gloomy days that followed on the heels of an uneventful *eid*.

"Yes! What's up? Calm down. You know I only picked up because you know how to deliver news. The lawyers and the rest can be quite untactful." She let out, mentally exhausted.

"The lawyer's office just called me. They did say that they couldn't reach you. They found out from Manu's sealed files that he is in the habit of suing people with deep pockets over banal things!" Taherah shrieked over the phone. "We got him! From what they said, it is probable and reasonably possible that he will drop the case."

"Ya Wajid!" Hajaratu praised. "Thank you for finding this dirt," Hajara sighed relieved. She said it more to Allah ﷺ than anyone else. "*Alhamdullilah…*"

"On another note, Salif and I are also getting married!" Taherah announced.

"Which Salif?"

"The same one you know."

"Salif, my chef!?"

"The same exact one…"

"Oh, you are very conniving, Dear Neece…" Hajaratu said, words failed her, but a laugh overpowering her. "Now that things are looking promising… life is short. I am going to call Tariq and propose to him!"

"Wow! Such boldness and confidence! Bring me back something from your honeymoon. I knew that you two were perfect for each other the minute I saw the looks you exchanged in my presence. I simply knew. Go for it, Auntie. I am with you. I look forward to seeing your in-laws hehe," she teased. "Marriage vibezzz," she squealed.

"And you have not stopped trying to match me with him," Hajaratu said, tauntingly in the receiver. Then, a deep throaty African laugh followed. "And don't annoy me with that in-laws talk. I am sure I will be able to handle them, if God wills. He is an orphan, but his uncle and his aunt are like parents to him. In most West-African cultures, the aunts and uncles usually give you in marriage, not your birth parents. Hopefully, I am younger than them." She said, dread filling her.

Hajaratu also worried about her side of her family who would treat her as if she was ruining a young's man life.

She imagined some of them saying, "Why do you want this poor youth to be cursed and die, too?" Like the decree of death was in her hand. In her opinion, her late husband simply died because his time was up.

"Don't worry, Auntie. You have at least 20 years before you are considered a really old lady in my books. Right now, you are just a Cougar! Bye!"

"The nerve of this kid!" Hajaratu said in shock, staring at her receiver with a dead tone beeping from the other side.

***

Hajaratu called Tariq. He picked up. She greeted him, and he responded to her peace greeting.

"I thought it would go to voicemail," she confessed. She was happy it didn't because she wasn't about to propose on a voicemail and the courage to call might never hit her again if he had not picked up. It was now or never.

"I wanted to hear your voice, so I picked up," Tariq confessed softly into the receiver.

There was a comfortable pause between them at that moment. It was thick with so many unsaid words of care. Her insides melted, so she mustered up courage to pour her heart out.

"Tariq."

"Yes, Hajar."

"I really like you, and I cannot imagine a life without you. Will you marry me?" the words were out of her mouth before she could start talking about Manu or otherwise rambling.

After proposing to Tariq, she wanted to hide. She reckoned that sometimes when you ask the Creator not to leave you to your devices, even for the blinking of an eye, he facilitates issues rapidly. There, she had easily said it. She had thought she would have more prelude leading to the actual proposal words that she will never be able to take back.

But Tariq reassured her. "I admire your courage! Of course, I will be elated to be your husband, it will solve so many problems for me emotionally."

She laughed at that. She knew he had erotic feelings towards her.

"Don't get me wrong, I am attracted to you, but you are a *Innaha kanat wa kanat*, like the Prophet ﷺ said about his first wife, May God be pleased with her."

Hajaratu smiled at the honor. "*Aameen. Alhamdullilah,* you have a lot of Prophetic qualities. These are the reasons why I want you, too."

Tariq told her that he would inform his uncle and aunt, and that they would send a delegation to her relatives. "People from Senegal are everywhere. I am sure some acquaintances, friends or even family in Ivory Coast can go see the elders in your family." He assured her.

"Or your relatives from Senegal can travel to Ivory Coast. We can cover the costs. Also, I don't want to get married right away."

"Why?!" Tariq exclaimed passionately. "I know that we have known each other for only eight months, and we have lived in closed quarters for four and half months or so, but we have that connection."

She laughed. "Exactly, you have all the qualities. You are marriage material, but I still think we should plan it out well. We shouldn't rush into it even though we have that urge we want to satisfy. Allah ﷻ is the patient."

"Fine…" he grumbled. "By the way, what did you do you with my suit?"

"I framed it," she retorted.

"No, seriously. Where is it?"

"You will get it after *nikah,* insha'Allah. I have taken it as hostage for now until we pass these high waters. It keeps me company, like my cat sometimes. Anyways, how about we plan the *nikah* just before next year's Ramadan. It will give us more time to get comfortable with each other's goals, routines, and whatnot."

"You are killing me…" Tariq moaned out of disappointment, and she teased him for dashing his hopes. "Plus, that cat hates me."

"She is my girlfriend, and she is jealous, ha!"

"For real! I have to work on her. She always drops dead things in front of my door."

Hajaratu laughed, "It might be how she shows her affection, by bringing you gifts."

"Hmm," is all he said. And a brief pause ensued.

She cleared her throat before landing the next question. "Have you been with a woman before?" she asked quite blankly.

"Yes, it was in my teenage years. I was going through a phase because of the loss of my parents. It was only once. I have not been active for over ten years."

"I am sorry to hear that. But see, one more year is nothing. You can handle it."

"How about you? When was the last time you were active?" he asked.

"Five years ago, when I became a widow," she said and paused again.

"Sorry about that," he said.

"Allah ﷻ gives and Allah ﷻ takes. *Alhamdullilah ala kulli haal.* I am happy."

Will you tell me about him one day?"

"It was an abusive marriage to a painter, so I rather not. Let's just leave it at that."

"No problem. I understand. Any children?"

"Yes, I have a son, but he is studying in England."

"Really? How old is he?"

"Nour is nine years old. He will come home during the summer, insha'Allah. We talk every night."

"Interesting! I would have never imagined since there is no picture of him anywhere. Now, I am nervous to know if he will like me. Why so far and why England?"

"It's a long story but the short version is that he is in a Muslim boarding school where he is memorizing Quran. That is why I said you have to really know me before we do this. And I really have to know you well, too. This is plenty of time for us to grow healthily since I can't give you children right away. Plus, we have to do *istikhara*."

"What if *istikhara* is not favorable?"

"Allah ﷻ doesn't tease people and leave them hanging. Khair insha'Allah."

"Khair insha'Allah," he added, too.

***

Tariq and Hajaratu Hilal got married in Sha'ban in the year that followed. They made plans to perform *umrah* together in the third week of Ramadan for double the reward and spent part of *eid* in Mecca Mukarramah, Madina al-Munawrah and the rest home with their relatives. Since the moon sighting varied across the *ummah*, they had five days of *eid* while also blissfully travelling and eating tasty food. While they were in Saudi Arabia, the bookish newlyweds visited the King Fahd Glorious Quran Printing Complex.

There, Hajaratu opened a Quran like she had seen him do during *tilawah* bonding time with the Codex.

His was a hand-written Codex from Timbuktu protected by a leather cover he had paid a fortune to get and hers was her great-great-great grandfather's Codex from seventeen century Mankono in West Africa.

That day, Hajaratu fell on Quran 30:21. The timing of this sign made her smile. Tariq leaned over to see what situation she brought to The Codex and his lips widened at the verse she was pointing at with her finger.

"And one of His signs is that He created for you spouses from among yourselves so that you may find comfort in them. And He has placed between you compassion and mercy. Surely in this are signs for people who reflect."

– Quran 30:21

THE END.

BOOK TWO: THE CRITERION

" The ˹true˺ servants of the Most Compassionate are

...

are˺ those who pray, "Our Lord! Bless us with ˹pious˺ spouses and offspring who will be the joy of our hearts, and make us models for the righteous."

— Quran 25:63-74

Table of Contents

Chapter 1

Afoussata

July/Muharram

THE BELL AT THE main door made its signature noise, and Afou knew she had company. So, she made her way to the front of the shop pausing the soap cutting task at hand. Inhaling the citrus scent of the sage batch of soaps, she exhaled soothingly. Soap making was always a healing experience for Afou. She enjoyed the patience it helped her build and the stress it helped her release as her hands being occupied allowed her brain to rest. All she did during soapmaking was mindful *dhikr*. She finally arrived at the front desk and noticed the client examining different products with interest. So, she greeted him first.

"Hello, welcome to our shop." The client lifted his face, and he returned the greeting still preoccupied.

"Hi."

"Let me know if you need anything," Afou said, intrigued by his suit on a Sunday. *He could be a church goer*, her conscience pointed out.

The customer simply nodded and brought a wrapped bar soap to his nose and closed his eyes with delight. She smiled at his satisfaction. Five minutes passed and he was still inspecting her products. So, Afoussata simply lifted her head in his

105

direction from time to time to see his progress within the scented shop. Finally, he approached the counter with his basket filled with a variety of cosmetics; soaps, lotions, gels, lip balms, salves, shampoos and bath salts. Afou knew customers could be carried away in her shop. So even though she widened her eyes at the man's purchase, she kept it professional.

"Would you like any gift packaging for these or would one bag suffice?" she asked and immediately she sensed hesitation on his face. So she added, "the client is king, so ask away."

"If it's not too much trouble, can you package them as gifts? They are intended for my friend's wedding favors. I can help since I am short on time." He let out a breath of relief as the words escaped his lips.

"Absolutely! Let me go grab the gift bags. I will be right back." Taking note of the colors he had picked for the cosmetics; she inferred the wedding had a lot of coral hues and the see through gold gift back she had could fit. They were festive and matched almost any occasion. When she returned, they agreed to make a goody bag comprised of bath salts, bar soap, and shampoos. And then another style of lip balms, salves, and lotions.

The order was about $200 without the packaging. They worked quickly and efficiently and within thirty minutes they were done.

"Alhamdullilah," she whispered under her breath as they walked out with the bags to his car.

"Alhamdulillah is right," the customer added, pointedly and finally introduced himself, "I'm Choualiyou but my friends call me Charles."

"Interesting," Afou replied, barely hiding her surprise. All this while, she took him for a non-Muslim man. Even his debit card supported her initial assessment of this man with an unusual name but unique enough for her to know the origin. She was a student of knowledge after all, and it was a name her folks used a lot. She always thought it was an African name until the name came up in one of her *seerah* classes, and she made the link with one of distant cousin she had always found peculiar. That was several years ago. The uncanny occurrence again just blew her away. So, all she said to herself was, "Ya Allah what are you trying to tell me? Please make it clear ya Mubeen."

"Nice to meet you Choualiyou. Sorry I zoned out a bit. Your name took me by surprise," she admitted.

"I can tell. I asked you a question you didn't hear."

"Which was?"

"What is your name dear sister?"

"I'm Afoussata. I go by Afou. Thank you for supporting our shop. Please come again."

"You're welcome, Insha'Allah. There is not a shortage of African weddings especially amongst young professionals like us."

"Right, take care," she agreed, smiling at his true comment.

She also knew he was different right then because their culture had a negative thing to say about gifting people things that end and smell good. Since he was defying convention with his choice, she smiled. *I like that.*
When she returned to her shop, she

uttered, "Ya Razzaq, thank you for a generous first customer. He tipped her a lot because she helped him expedite the crisis his friend was facing with the guests' favors. Apparently, the order of chocolate they had planned never arrived and they had to come up with a solution and her shop was the only shop opened so bright and early on this Sunday morning in this particular small town on the outskirts of McKinney. She ran the shop with her younger sister. Her sister made soaps, too, but took care of the books mainly. They loved to work together and sometimes with her sister's children and her son.

Chapter 2

Choualiyou

CHARLES LEFT THE SHOP relieved but with a nagging thought. The only reason he was pulled in that shop for last minutes gift ideas was because on the shop's name;

Kolan

~Savonerie & Homemade Cosmetics~

He spoke a little French since his parents were immigrants from French West Africa. But they definitely made sure he spoke his mother's tongue at an early age. It was the default language of their home. French was only spoken as a backup language when they forgot the name of something in Dioula or Bambara. And Charles could bet anything that Kolan meant soap. He was intrigued by this shop from the get-go and the shop owner as well. He found her polite and to the point. Normally, people exuded an array of emotions that he matched. Afou like she said she was called, was neutral; platonic even. He could hardly pick up on her vibes because she seemed so guarded so he matched her vibe; polite indifference. Besides he was there to salvage a wedding not to look for a daughter-in-law for his insistent mother. He had found a shea butter and strawberry body scrub he couldn't wait for his mom to try. He even found some cute black soaps. His mother loved black soap, and she was very picky about who made it. *Ya Allah let her love these cosmetics*, he prayed inwardly.

Choualiyou returned to the wedding venue hopeful and ready for the ceremony to commence. The venue was in Princeton, Texas. The *walimah* had a farm vibe to it. The Ghanaian wedding planner recommended this ranch taking into account the wedding list kept growing and they were having issues stabilizing it. Tell an African they can't come to a wedding and you have won an enemy for life.

"That way if there is no room to sit, they will sit on a tabouret and feel like right at home," an Aunty said during the wedding's preparations. It was a messed up logic but they had no other alternatives. Many of his folks children had graduated in the surrounding cities such as Commerce, Arlington, Austin, Dallas, Waco, San Antonio, and Houston. So, the immigrant population was definitely present and visiting each other especially during this summer. The *nikkah* had been performed the year before but the *walimah* had to be postponed so that many of their folks from overseas could attend.

Choualiyou arrived at the barn fifteen minutes later and parked on the unpaved road like the rest of the cars. Then he ran to the barn to meet the rest of the team, setting up the tables for the guests.

"Welcome back oh!" The Ghanaian wedding shouted. "Please tell me you saved the day Charles!" she prodded.

"Let me show you!" he responded.

"Amazing! Let's put them on the tables. They will go well with the white and coral roses on each table and the silverware." Then she glanced up at the stringed lights in the ceiling of the barn, silently echoing her sentiment with the ceiling's decorations.

"I agree. The coral napkins also work with the gifts." Choualiyou said and started with the first table next to him draped in a white tablecloth on which the center piece was a bouquet of light coral and white roses. The glasses were transparent, and the plates were white, too."

They worked quickly, because the guests were supposed to arrive around 11 a.m. It was 9:45 a.m.

"We will bring the cake when the guests are here. I don't want it to melt in this Texas heat!"

***

"Bro! You saved the day with these party favors; Fatimah says thank you. *Alhamdullilah*." Abdul Karim let out a breath of relief. "If you weren't a diplomat and that is my nice way of saying politician, you could have explored wedding planning." The groom added, laughing. *Tu as raté ta vocation!*"

"Here we go again with the event planning stuff," Charles huffed. "Dude, my job is "technically event planning and damage control". So, this is just up my street. *Walaye*, my parents would have doubted my manhood if I chose that career. You know how Immigrants parents are," Charles said in the receiver. "Anyway, enjoy your night at the hotel with your bride. We'll catch up later."

"No problem man, thanks again. Ee

111

Baraqa. Allah troman gnouman diman, ameen. God bless you and give you a great life companion, too. Aameen. Don't stay too long over there tying up loose ends. You were a spectacular best man. And oh, my sister Halimah and Fatimah wants to go to that shop please. So, let's plan a trip there insha'Allah before we leave this small town."

"*Aameen*, don't mention it. I will be delighted to take you there." His heart made a weird flip he couldn't place at the mention of going back to the soaperie and possibly seeing the intriguing soap owner again.

Adjoua, was a competent wedding planner. And she said with her heavy and noticeable accent, "Councilman, if you were not busy with the town, I wouldn't have minded a business partner like you." Then, she gave him a motherly smile. "My daughter is single by the way."
"Aunty, thank you for the compliment. My heart is taken."

"By whom? You had no woman with you at the wedding."
"Aunty, we do things a bit differently."

"I know! My friend Qari is Muslim. Yet, you look a bit liberal."

He winced at the comment. *Really?*

Interesting. He always thought of himself as a decent Muslim. He tried not to take offense and changed the subject.
"Auntie, if there are issues in the Ghanaian community that you think I help with, please let me know. Also, please let me know if you need help in

your future weddings. I can volunteer if my time allows God willing.

"I will take up on that offer!" she beamed at his response.

He wasn't sure if it was to show off her daughter or if she will actually need him. Either way, he said his goodbyes and left the ranch for his place. At least she was upfront. He remembers about two years ago when he visited Ivory Coast. Every auntie who came to greet his family because he was visiting home came with her daughter. This was a subtle way to say, *my daughter is available for your son if he is interested.* It was a wild experience for him. Thinking back of it at the moment made him puff in laughter.

His father had already left with his Mom for Prosper, Texas. They owned a cozy home there. The days' events kept playing in his mind. One of distant uncles had made the trip and called him by a nickname that no one used anymore in his family; Leemamy (the Imam).

"When are you getting married Leemamy?" the elder had hollered when Choualiyou passed by his table to check on the guests of that table.

"When Allah ﷻ decides Uncle," Choualiyou replied with a chuckle. "Only you call me that these days."

"Don't be ashamed of your name. Sadly, very few people know the meaning of your name today. If it wasn't that your grandfather insisted, his name would behave been forgotten by now. He took pride in the name of this early and renown

Muslim Imam he was given by the village *ulamas* of his time. Give thanks!"

Choualiyou winced at the public roast, "OK Uncle, y'all please let us know if you need anything." Then, he moved to the next guests. Being roasted in public is normal for his folks so he quickly made his peace with the debate he involuntarily instigated.

He was happy for Abdul Kareem and had no interesting leads at the moment. Many non-Muslim women he came across could fill the spot but the thought that they weren't IT stopped him on many occasions. He was looking for something he, himself, wasn't sure what it was.

Chapter 3

Choualiyou

CHOUALIYOU RETURNED TO WORK the day after. He was working on a policy for international students having been in a community where many of his peers had to pay humongous out-of-state tuition fees in order to pursue their education in this new land. Many had to drop because they couldn't pay. It saddened him many brilliant minds he knew come came in America with a bright future, good grades, top of their schools and much decorated for their academic achievements back home didn't make it in this land of opportunities simply because tuitions fees became an hindrance. *Naudhubillah.* He was grateful that he was born in the USA. Some Africans made it regardless of the costs but they had to work and try to maintain their good brand so they could land a scholarship so they start paying in-state tuitions. If they couldn't achieve that, they had to take ridiculous loans to make it. Another issue was the working permit, it was hard to get a working permit as a student. You had to build a strong case that warranted permission to work outside campus; family unforeseen circumstances, etc. While the success stories are many and few in between, so are the failure stories. So, his goal was to seek the city's councilors and also the neighboring cities' help so that a fund/grant that can be setup for desperate cases. Choualiyou had named the policy in progress US Committee for International Students aka USCIS-F1. So that it is not confused with the immigration and naturalization agency of homeland security, he added F1 at the end since international students have a F1 immigration status. Choualiyou also knew the critics to his policy all too well.

"Don't you have to show that you can pay for the tuitions before the school extends you a I-20?" The critics would ask.

"Yes, but--" would start Choualiyou but they will stop listening at that point.
"Then, we don't see the need of this new policy. You guys bring it upon yourselves."

It was often pointless to let them know that many families always thought they could handle it because of their considerable savings; only to realize that money goes out faster than it comes in. The narrative they were exposed to was that it is easy to find a job in a US. So, even if they fall short at one point, their children would be able to work and wing it. When parents send their children overseas because they are tired of the recurrent strikes in African universities and the normal political instability, the unsaid statement is this: *the whole family is counting on you.* That pressure is also enough to motivate or demotivate F1 because of the new weight he or she has to now shoulder. Once a critic of his policy said, "If your people signed an affidavit saying that they could afford school why do you bother us with this issue? You guys have great universities there, too. Why don't they stay there and pursue their schooling in peace?"

Choualiyou was so aggravated that he retorted, "Your people in the project or minority neighborhoods that are accepted in private Ivy Leagues schools, don't you praise them for their ambitions and their will to want to carve a path for themselves and their families? Why don't they stay in the schools of their communities or only go to Black colleges?"

The critic had no answer to that. Choualiyou had hit common ground and after that conversation while the critic didn't support his cause, he no longer opposed Choualiyou trying to carve out a path for his community as well.

Chapter 4

Afoussata

THE NEXT DAY, ON Monday, Afou dropped her son at school and drove to Downtown Dallas to teach an intensive summer program. She worked in a minority school in downtown; the school mainly catered to Blacks and Hispanics. She taught French. This was her day job. She didn't enjoy the commute but it paid the bills and put food on the table.   *Alhamdullilah.* The traffic was usually heavy on Highway 75 but she normally arrived on time even with the usual slowness and backup so she didn't fret. She simply did her usual mindful *dhikr.* Once at school, she parked her car and made her way inside the school. She treated other colleagues on the way there and replied to the greetings of other students who addressed her.

"Good morning Ms. Timité," said one student and a   math   teacher.

"Good morning Pauline," she said to the student and then addressed the teacher, "Morning Michele. See you at lunch."

"Alright, see you in the teacher's lounge later."

"Bonjour Mademoiselle Timité," another student said as Afou continued to make her way to her class.

"Bonjour Valarie, comment ça va?" Afou replied and engaged the student because she knew Valarie enjoyed their brief conversations. "Très bien."

Valarie was originally from New Orleans, so she always spoke French or patois to Afou because this year she wasn't taking French.

In her class, Afou put her purse away, shove her lunch bag in her small personal fridge in a corner of the class and left her work bag on the table. Her class had posters of many French landmarks including the Eiffel Tower. She also had the map that highlighted the French speaking countries around the world. Many these countries were African because they had been French colonies. Her homeland amongst it; Ivory Coast.

The day unfolded as she covered and taught topics ranging from French Grammar, Conjugation, Orthography, Conversational French and much more. At lunch, she removed her lunch bag from the ice box and went to the teacher's break room. Teachers were engrossed in different conversations. Some brought lunch and other had trays from the cafeteria. Once her cursive look of room the spotted Michele, she went toward her direction and sat facing her.

"Hey," Michele said first.

"Hi," returned Afou, lethargic. "How was morning?"

"It was OK. About half of them did their homework so it can be a challenge to teach if they are not prepared. But anyway, I am doing my best. How about you?"

"Conjugation class was harder on them today. I pray they get it soon."

"They will," Michele encouraged. "What's new aside that? How is the shop?"

"The shop is good. We had a great tipper yesterday," Afou said, dropping her face as if she was trying to hide her emotions. She picked at her salad with her fork dejected. When she finally took a bite and the emotion she was trying to contain passed, she lifted her face and faced her colleague.

"Was he cute?" asked Michele.

Afou shrugged her shoulders.

"What was that? What are you hiding Afou?" Michele asked inquisitively.

"Nothing!" Afou replied a bit too forcefully. Michele assessed her with squinted eyes for a minute, then added, " Time will tell."

Afou just smiled, staring into her salad and changed the subject. "When are opening your papery and stationary shop?"

"Nice way to deflect the conversation. My mom thinks I should open a bakery instead. I don't know what to do."

"Just pray and let the decision come to you," Afou advised.

"I have been praying but the decision I chose might not please my mom. I like both ideas but baking is more her dream," Michele said, divided.

"Well, if you want blessings, you go with her choice. Then perhaps because of your sincerity, God will open a door for you later if He wishes.

"Hmm, I will think about it. On another note, you are still eating a salad. I guess your sister didn't cook for you to pack today."

"You know I don't cook anymore. My future husband will do all the cooking God willing."

"If you aren't Muslim, I would said you are high again," Michele pinned.

They laughed and continued to chat until the time to return to their respective classes. When it was time for *zhur salat*, Afou gave the students an assignment and excused herself for ten minutes to connect to her Lord. She prayed for the ummah of prophet Muhammad , ﷺ for Palestine, Syria, Sudan, Congo, anywhere there was unrest, even domestically. She also asked Allah ﷻ to guide her and rectify all her affairs and her family's. Finally, Afou asked Allah ﷻ to make her mother happy and never sad, to grant her *Jannah al Firdaus* to shower His mercy on her, to always give her courage and never let be afraid, to accept all of her mother's actions; the small ones and the big ones. Then, Afou added a long *aameen* and closed her *salat* with Surah Fatiha and she returned to work.

An hour later, the students were dismissed, and her class was empty. She tied up loose ends and left the school by 3:30 pm :30 pm and hoped to pray *asr* in McKinney after picking up her son since it was the summer. Prayer times were longer. During the winter, she had to pray *asr* shortly after dismissal before driving back home. Otherwise, she would find herself dangerously close to praying *asr* at a *makruh* time because *magrib* was around 5:20-30

121

pm during the winter. That stress didn't last long because mid-December, school was normally out, and *Wa Allahu yuqadiru layla wa nahar*—Allah, alone, keeps a precise measure of the day and the night. So, trying to remember what was outside her control helped her rid herself of the stress she unnecessarily put upon herself. *He is Merciful.* She always reminded herself.

Chapter 5

Choualiyou

THE SATURDAY THAT FOLLOWED Kolan received a delegation of West Africans because of their telltale prints

ready to "ransack" the shop's goodies. Amongst them an elderly woman ready to look down on the shop owner who became the main attraction in her family and guests' home.

"Hello, welcome to our shop," Satou short for Nafissatou extended beaming at the new clientele. She was immediately approached by a young professional with questions.

"I was here last week, and another woman helped me. Is she here today?"

"Oh, my sister is in town but she is at a tradeshow today. I can help you or I can give her location so you can go see what she has to sell over there," Satou replied, still smiling. She had her two-year-old bouncing on her hips. Her six-year-old son was coloring on a nearby table next to a soap making artisan station they used for their monthly team building classes catered to the public, couples, and high school science classes."

Charles turned his attention to his party and spoke in Dioula to inform them that Afou was at another location; up-Town. Satou immediately jumped in the conversation feeling at home and approached the group and showed her loving respects to the frowning elderly who surprised by the mindfulness of Satou defrosted her mood. Then, she talked the heads of the young women accompanying Charles and Abdul Karim. In a matter of minutes, the women had grabbed more products recommended by Satou; the marketer of the shop. Her enthusiasm was contagious.

Satou gave Charles a flyer of their upcoming appearances around town. Charles promised himself to stop at one of these pop-up shops to gauge the intriguing Afou a little more. The elder woman conceded that the technique of black soaping used by the sisters was unmatched and that they were worth their salts.

"Thank you *Ounan*, Mom," Satou beamed, delighted   at   the   comment.
"My best friend, Charles' Mom missed out. Next time insha'Allah."

Chapter 6

Choualiyou

August/Safar

ANOTHER MONTH PASSED BEFORE Charles was able to set his eyes on Afou. *Am I stalking her?* he asked himself, not sure why he wanted to see her so much. Every time he used her products in the shower, he felt relaxed and dreamy. *To tell her you like her products.* His conscience pointed. Heh, I could leave a review online to tell her that. No, there is more to it, and I cannot put my finger on it. I like her but is it an infatuation or something more serious?

Afou was pleasantly surprised to see Charles again after his gang descended upon them about a month ago and demanded to see her. She was amazed at the boldness of his folks and amused at the same time. It felt like they couldn't believe the quality of the soap making from the motherland exported to the land of opportunities. She was thankful Satou set them straight gently and with tact like she knew how to do.

Aside from that, she had enjoyed his proximity as they worked diligently while bagging cosmetics that fateful Sunday morning. His perfume was light but memorable. And that scent disturbed her for weeks because she had a thing for distinct smells. But because she was doing a lot of heart work, she had to constantly remember Allah ﷻ to protect her heart from unreasonably attaching it to a tempting peculiar customer with a peculiar given name.

"What do you do for a living?" she had asked curiously when he returned with his mom, and they found themselves about non-soap related matters.

"I am a councilman for the City of Dallas. Our community is so prominent here and many of our issues were neglected while I was growing up that it was only fair that I try to make a change within my own community.
"Nice, masha'Allah."

"Do you want to see what I do to help you visualize better?"

"Sure," she replied, interested.

After watching the charismatic YouTube video, she asked, "how do protect your heart from self-amazement entering in it?"

"It's an occupational hazard," he replied, shrugging.

Afou winced and he realized he might have said the wrong thing because he said next, "Wrong answer huh?"

"Definitely. For your relationship with Allah ﷻ, yourself, and people in your life. *Kabir* belongs to Allah ﷻ alone. Self-care is important, and if your cup is empty, you can't effectively and efficiently pour in others. I am just saying."

"Wow, deep... I regret showing you my work, lol!"

"*Tazkiyyah* is important to me. Because--" she got cut off as his mom returned from perusing other stalls. "So, I never told you why my friend was frowning at your shop last time."

"Do tell Ounan."

"She was 'enraged' that people said that I suddenly looked younger than her. Your face masks Choualiyou bought made the trick. She normally gets complimented all the time because she is older than me."

That tickled Afou a little. She tried to avoid full blown laughs since she learned that Rasul ﷺ didn't do Kakah.

When she stopped, he said, "You should smile more."

Afou simply pursed her lips amusingly.

 Charles' Mom bought more strawberry scrubs. "What did you think of her?" he asked his mom on the way back.

"She was polite but may be she is not your type."

"Mom, you don't know my type," he said, laughing.

"Fine, only Allah ﷺ knows."

Chapter 7

Choualiyou
September/Rabbi Al-Awwal

CHARLES HAD MET A young father by the name of Ahmadou who studied civil engineering in Ivory Coast and won the green card lottery. When Ahmadou arrived in the US, he was full of hope, only to find himself doing small jobs here and there and supporting his larger family back home; he was the eldest child of his family. At the time he was single, now he was married with two children. Ahmadou worked day and night to support himself, his parents, and siblings. He never found time to resume his studies in the land of opportunities because he never caught a break with bills and emergencies from all sides that assaulted him from the get-go. He is been trying to get into the IT field because he heard it was better but now he couldn't afford the tuitions because the hard labor he had subjected his young body had taken a toll on him. This always reminded Choualiyou of verse 68 of Surah Yasin that said; *And whoever We grant a long life, We reverse them in development. Will they not then understand?* Choualiyou didn't know how to help Ahmadou because he had the problem as other immigrants but he wasn't F1. He had a green card. The country simply repatriated the older working force that was undocumented and replaced with a documented and overqualified workforce. He read once a social post during Black History Month that said, "They didn't steal slaves. They stole Scientist, Doctors, Architects, Astronomers, Teachers, Entrepreneurs, Fathers, Mothers, Sons, Daughters, etc. & made them slaves." He agreed. Same dog, new tricks. Ahmadou had felt victim to that trick. He was overqualified but found himself with a bright future once he arrived in "the land of opportunities."

Chapter 8

Nafisatou

October/Rabbi Al-Akhir

"I'M LEAVING," SATOU YELLED over to grab the attention of his sister. "Come lock behind me. I will let know when I am home."

Afou appeared next to her a few moments later with her son. She hugged Satou and kissed her cheeks. "Let us know when you are home." Satou nodded. She could see her sister's husband outside through the window waiting for his family to exit the store. Afou waved at him, and he waved back with a smile. Hudhaifa said bye to his cousins and added, "Good night Auntie."

"Good night Baba," she replied, tenderly looking at him with kind eyes. She gave him her full attention with her two-year-old on her hip as usual. "Take good care of your Mom, OK?"

Hudhaifa nodded, proudly, up for the challenge. "That's my boy," Auntie Satou said. "See you tomorrow," her son Losseni, a variant of the name Hussain, let out. And the parents added insha'Allah on cue before chuckling.

About fifteen minutes later, the text came that Satou had made safely home with her family. They lived in Princeton, Texas, too.

Their shop was in an old marketplace with cobblestone streets, next to a small variety of artisan shops lined up next to each other's on each side of the road. All the shops around were decorated with a fall theme with pumpkins and hay displayed at the shops' doors or in the streets. Even the windows had some kind of indication that it was fall and Thanksgiving was coming.

Chapter 9

Afoussatou

November/Jumada I

EVERY BEGINNING OF THE month, Afou delivered the local hotels' orders of small bar soaps, shampoos and conditions. Soon after, came the regular clients came along with the tourists. Then, Thanksgiving Day and break was upon the community. Black Friday was busy. While The Timités didn't celebrate the national holiday, their customers and the tourists expected bargain prices, so they indulged the community.

That Monday that followed, Noel's decorations were already up and at the speed of lightning. "These people don't play around with their holidays," Afou told her sister, laughing. A well-lit pagan tree had grown at the roundabout overnight with its shining garlands and ornaments.

Still in conversation with her sister, Afou added, "Remember the people of prophet Shubaib *aleihi salam* used to worship trees?"

"Yeah..." Satou replied, traipsing on her words as if she did not want to start that conversation.

"This time of the year now gives me that vibe; it's uncanny."

"If you are not close to God, you are close to Shaytan and all this, is the devil's work. Remember, he promised to beautify evil for us. No doubt, the cities are beautiful until after Valentine's Day. All *shirk*; idolatry," Satou chimed in. Her mild attempt at avoiding the conversation was pointless. The words tumbled out her mouth anyway.

"Exactly!" Afou agreed and they continued working, lamenting the plight of real trees around town who had also been taken in hostage for unreligious and pagan decoration. Their trunks were dressed with string lights. "If the trees could speak to us, they would affirm the words of Quran, 'Everything in the earth and sky worship God'."

Chapter 10

Choualiyou
December/Jumada II

ONCE A MONTH, CHOUALIYOU had made it a point to go "restock" at Kolan. He wasn't sure if she was excited to see him but he was definitely excited to see his platonic demeanor. With Afou, he came to the conclusion that he enjoyed her company because he didn't have to put on a show or match her energy; a thing that could be so draining. She was always constant emotions wise; she either knew how to hide her emotions wells or had simply mastered nonchalance; in a good way. They were now in December since their first meeting in July at the shop. Ramadan was three months away if God willed. He wondered what Ramadan would look like with this woman becoming the center of his thoughts with each day that passed.

Afoussata

Afou avoided year-end parties with all her might because they were disguised Christmas parties. This year like every year, she was also ready to dodge it. She went outside the school to her car during the time she knew the teachers' lounge will be celebrating a pagan event. When enough time passed, Afou went to her class and noticed that an

Ethiopian teacher who wasn't Muslim was also trying to dodge the party, too. Afou classed her perhaps as an orthodox Christian; a thing very common in Ethiopia until this day. Birthdays were also not allowed in that teacher's faith.

They both returned to their classes relieved until the principal barged in on them and took them hostage much like all the trees around the town forced to partake in a celebration their Lord and Creator had not made permissible for them.

She said deceitfully, "You need to join everyone. Come on! It's not a Christmas party nor a birthday party. I have an address that you need to be present for."

It was begrudgingly that the two self-outcasted teachers joined the teacher's lounge. While they couldn't disobey a direct order from their boss, they could decline to eat anything pertaining to the event. And that was exactly what they did.

The email that was sent a week earlier, mentioning the event had clearly said it was a birthday celebration for many teachers who had birthdays recently combined with a Christmas party. And when Afou and the Ethiopian teacher joined the room, a gift exchange game was taking place. Ten minutes later, the principal addressed her subjects about the year in review and the upcoming goals for the new year. At 2pm, Afou excused herself to go pray. Michele gave her wink on the way out. She winked back. They knew it was her cue. Afou had fasted that day so that she could easily avoid the temptation of eating. She planned but the schemes of the devil won that day. In the grand scheme of things, she knew it was the will of Allah. Nothing happens except if he allows it. It was just a small win for Iblis. *Alhamdullilah ala kulli halal.*

A few more days passed, and they were on winter break. And Afou found herself deep in her thoughts. *It's mid-month, Choualiyou should be stopping by. Eek! I hope he like the new soaps we made with baobab powder.* She paced and back and forth in the shop. Every time, the door opened she rushed to see if it was him at last.

"Sit down, you are making me nervous. He will come insha'Allah," Satou said, mischievously.

Afou widened her eyes in horror.

"What?! You thought you weren't transparent? I see or recognize patterns remember? You get anxious like that you, you my calm sister and leveled headed sister every mid-month."

Since Afou lost her voice, she was still in shock from her sister's comment. She kept staring, bewildered, chest heaving at her indiscretion. So, Satou continued her assessment, "We both noticed his I picked up on your habits. You were a crisper hijab around this time of the month. You groomed yourself more, etc. etc. Etc. Honestly, I am happy to see some life in you after your devastating divorce."

"*Astaghfirullah...*" is all she could mustered last and hid her face his palms before slumping on a nearby pouf of the store dejectedly.

Satou got up from behind the counter to come rub the back of sister soothingly.

"When are you going to introduce him to Hudhaifa?"

"Perhaps, I should do that next time he comes so if he serious we will know. And I can see if this need to nipped at the bud?"

"I think that's a great idea."

When Choualiyou arrived that week, she was ready to put her plan in action. Expecting the worse, she was curt and not on her best behavior. After the usual greeting exchange, they normally had, she spoke first.

"I want you meet someone."

"OK..."

She peered strangely at him because of his reluctance. Then, she swiftly went to stand at bottom of the stair and called up, "Hudhaifa honey, please come down."

A few minutes later, a mixed boy of about ten years old made his way down the stairs.

When he joined his mom, he stood next to her expectantly. "Honey, remember when I asked you if you wanted to meet Mommy's friend?"

The boy nodded. "Okay, he is here and at the counter. Can you say s*alam*?"

So Hudhaifa extended s*alams* to Choualiuou.

"*Wa aleikum salam waramatullahi wabarakatuhu* young man. How are you?"

"I am good," her son replied confidently, head high staring at the councilman.

"What grade are you in?"

"I am fourth grade."

"Wow, you must smart Masha'Allah."

Hudhaifa shrugged while his mother had a nervous smile. "Anyway, nice to meet you. Mom, can I go back upstairs?"

"Of course, thank you for coming down," she said and kissed the middle of his curly hair. He gave her a hug back before dashing back upstairs.

"Nice kid. Is your son right?" he said as soon as they were alone.

"Yes. I am divorced. We live upstairs and I usually ask him not to come down during business hours. Anyway, Is that a deal breaker for you?" she asked, apprehensive off his response.

Charles remained quiet. When he finally spoke, "Maybe. Is my order ready?"

"Yes," she matched his cutting and sharp tone.

Then, she checked out his order in silence, and he left.

She slumped in the chair behind her with a heart full of emotions. Shattered. Devastated at the sudden loss of her favorite client and potential love interest. This is why you don't mix business and pleasure, she told herself bitterly. Then she added *alhamdulillah ala kulli haal*. Next, she called Satou and recounted her the stilted conversation.

"Wow, at least he was kind of straightforward."

"That was rude. That said, I had an attitude the minute he walked in already expecting the worse. I couldn't control my emotions today. *Astaghfirullah*."

"It's going to be an ice cream night," she said to herself, half-crying and laughing at herself.

Chapter 11

Afoussatou

TWO HOURS AFTER HE left the shop, Choualiyou called Kolan and Afou picked up.

"I'm sorry for the way I reacted tonight to you introducing your son to me. I was taken by surprise," he confessed, after the customary *salams*.

"We are adults, and I had to do something to either make or break whatever is going on between us."

"That was brutal," he said, laughing nervously.

"So, what are you looking for in a spouse?" Afou asked straight up. The time for serious discussion had arrived. They had delayed it long enough. "Wow, you are aggressive today," he pointed out.

"I don't any man to waste my time and lead me to approach *zina*."

"Fair point. What are you looking in a spouse?" he asked instead.

"Besides the mandatory faith requirement, I just want a want that can cook."

"What else?" he inquired.

"That it."

Choualiyou remained silent knowing it was his turn to spill the beans. Afou cleared her throat to hint that she was waiting for his response, but he remained silent for a little more before finally letting out the difficult words.

"I had envisioned a partner who had not been married yet, not a virgin to be clear but without any children."

The sharp breath of air that Afou took made him say, "Please don't get me wrong. You're amazing but I am not sure if I can fill this cup. It requires a lot of work. And I am thinking I am not well-equipped for the challenge your situation poses to me."

"I can understand that. You are a Politician for sure. You deescalated the issue so easily. I was going to give you a piece of my mind because of the conations and the implications of your first response but then again, I was taught not to argue with anyone. I'm a kran môgô dé, a student of knowledge."

Choualiyou

Her comment about being a student of knowledge intrigued but he didn't think it was right to ask about that. Did she mean like she studied in the village *madrasa*? He had a hard time picturing it. Did they have such institutes in the US? If so, it would be nice. Perhaps, he would also follow the footsteps of his ancestors and live up to his name at last like the elders wished. He knew from the little he gathered in Sunday school while growing up that knowledge is a duty upon every Muslim, and he had the bare minimum to pray and observe the pillars of faith. He had completed four pillars of Islam. He had not performed *umrah* or *hajj* and he wasn't lacking the means to go. As more questions popped up in his mind, he did his best to put a stop them for assaulting his mind. Then, he called his mom. She was an excellent sounding board for him.

"She is nice, but she is a single mom." Charles said dejectedly to his mom.

"Like I said before, maybe she is not your type. All the other boxes check off except the fact that she is divorced."

"Plus, she wants a man that cooks because she is already cooking soaps and traumatized from her first marriage where she was cooking five course meals daily to please him," he added.

"It will come all down to compromises," his mother said, knowingly. "She is still young, and you are about the same age. Both of your criteria can be resolved. One of the criterion one that doesn't compromise on, is faith.

Chapter 12

THE LOCAL *MASJID* SHE attended had a women's retreat twice a year; in January and in July to a Spanish speaking country. Afou had mentioned it to Michele Gonzalez. "Dude, I have been talking to you about Islam for a while now, this is the perfection occasion now that school is out to check it out."

She had said the same thing to Michele back in April of last year for the June's trip to Spain. Michele was saving for her cupcakes shop, so she said that she will try maybe in January to go to Costa Rica.

With the Choualiyou's ordeal, and the hole she felt like it was time to recharge. Satou and Afou left the children with her sister's husband and their parents for one week and went on a girl's trip to recharge. Their mother who lived in Plano was happy to lend a hand. After Satou explained to their mom that Afou had been a bit invested in a man, Mrs. Timité felt sad for her daughter Afou whom she wanted to remarry. So, she was for a rejuvenated trip.

After all, Michele couldn't go this time, too. Afou was bummed but prayed that Allah ﷺ guide her friend and colleague to this beautiful *deen*.

Mrs. Timité

Afou's father was a very tacit man. After some convincing from his wife, he agreed to run Kolan with his wife while his children go on a 'spiritual self-care journey.' "I will only great the customers and you can deal with all the chatty customers and ring them out while I read my newspaper and hang out with grandchildren."

And he was not joking. That is exactly what he did. Both were retired. So, one week running a shop wasn't taking them from any major daily activities. They got to see their grandchildren daily and that was a major plus for them.

After running the shop successfully for close to five days, Mrs. Timité remarked something peculiar. A customer she had helped two days in a row showed up again as if he was looking for something else. So, on the sixth night since the departure of their daughters, she picked her husband's brain, starting with an endearing term used in their culture.

"Ngôtchè--Big Brother, have you noticed a clean-cut man come to the shop several times this week to buy cosmetics since you sit by the door? There is no way he used all of these soaps he purchased." "It's a season of gifting. Leave the customers alone," the man replied, annoyed. He was trying to follow the news on the TV late in their room after they had closed the shop.

"Stop being obtuse," she snapped. Her purposely aggressive tone got his attention this time because he flipped his head in her direction in shock. "Fine, I noticed him. What about him?"

"Do you think we should call the cops next time he comes, or do you think he is safe?"

"Oh my God *Mamh*-Mother, don't blow things out of proportion. He is harmless."

"Are you sure? What are you not telling me?"

He removed his glasses and stared at his wife of thirty years for a moment before speaking again.

"One of those days, while I was sitting by the door, Hudhaifa was with me as we were having some bonding time. Since their moms don't allow them in the shop, I allow it. That's what grandparents do, veto." She squinted her eyes so he could stop going into tangents. "Anyway, one day the young man came and recognized Afou's son. They chatted a bit and Hudhaifa introduced him as 'Mommy's friend.' And we both know she doesn't have any male friend. It can only be that man she is uncentered about lately."

"Hmm," is all Mrs. Timité, the wheel turning in her mind now.

"Do you think he is looking for her?"

"It's possible." Her husband said, shrugging, resuming his previous activity; watching the news.

The next day, when the phone rang at the same time it had all the previous days, and when she had picked up, the caller hung up she was quicker with her words, "Afou is on trip. Can I take a message?"

The caller didn't hang up this time. He simply whispered his thanks before hanging up.

"These grownups are acting like teenagers," she said, shaking her head, in disbelief. "If you can't move on without her, just tell her!" she added with an irritated tone.

Chapter 13

The Katib
February/Shaban

AFOU AND SATOU HAD returned from their trip about three weeks ago glowing and ready to keep striving in their respective lives. Their mother quickly volunteered to pick them up from the airport, and she was already filling up their ears with the tales of the mysterious Choualiyou the minute they were comfortably sitting and had exchanged customary greetings. Afou and Satou just exchanged puzzled looks in the car. Afou sat next to her mom in the front and Satou sat in the back next her daughter's empty car seat. "Wait Mom, you mean Councilman Choualiyou Diarrassouba?"

"Yes! You didn't tell us he was Dioula! Your father and I criticized him in our language not knowing it. *Astaghfirullah.*"

"Oh my God, did you say anything inflammatory about him?" Satou asked rapidly?

"Well...it wasn't too bad. He can take it," she answered, shrugging. A mix of guilt and satisfaction in her demeanor. The girls just at her driving, amazed and equally. "Sis, you picked a guy with two big names; L'Imam and The Lion King with the Great Soul." Satou noted with a side eye.

Afou raised her hands in the air in defeat, laughing. "Allahu Abkar!" is all she said.

Once at home, they cooled off for a bit and then they handed their families members gifts they had brought from the trip.

"Your Mom and I called your 'boyfriend' a skinny tall tree in Dioula," Mr. Timité let out as he perused his fridge magnet nonchalantly. "That will teach him to treat our daughter like a second-class single mom."

"*Subhanallah*!" Afou exclaimed. "Y'all can be petty." And the whole family laughed.

"We said that to him as he was towering over us, and we had offered him a seat because he wanted to talk to us. Then, when he fully introduced himself, we realized he wasn't our cousin--a Black African American--he was an African. And not just any African; a Dioula. It was wild after what we had just said to him."

Satou fell from her chair to the floor, laughing. "It gets better," her dad added. "I said Diarrassouba? He nodded. "So, you speak Dioula?" He replied, "I was born here but I speak Dioula and Bambara perfectly.

Your mom said, 'Get out of here!' like the expression. She was surprised. She didn't actually mean for him to leave but she used an expression she rarely used to my surprise. So, he got to leave him.

Anyway, after all the miscommunication and missteps were out of the way, he asked for your hand in marriage." The dad deadpanned. "Get out of here!" said Satou in shock.

***

So, Shaban found them in heavy Ramadan preparations with the community along with *nikkah* preparations for Choualiyou and Afou. The plan was perform *umrah* during spring break in order to add *barakat* to the union. Hudhaifa went with the newly married couple. They were now a family, and he needed to be part of the *barakah seeking,* too.

So, they got married a week before Ramadan and like fate would have it, the order of the wedding cake and the cupcakes fell through as the *walimah* was scheduled in less than five hours in Prosper, at his family's home.

"What do we do?" Mrs. Timité asked, panicking. While every pore of Afou screamed bridezilla mode, she stilled herself with mindful *dhikr*. I'm calling Michele. She can help us *bithinillah*. So, she picked up her phone and placed the call.

After a few rings, Michele picked up.

"Hi Michele."

"Hi Mama. What's up. Is everything ok?"

"Remember my good tipper from several months back?"

"Yes..."

"I am getting married to him."

"What?!"

"That's not all. I need a baker asap. The company that was supposed to deliver the cake had an unforeseen problem. I need cupcakes and a cake like prompto. My guests will be here in less than five hours."

"So, you were going to get married without telling me or inviting me?"

"Please be mad at me another day. I beg you."

"Fine. Give me the address. My mom and I will be there in less than sixty minutes. You are lucky, I live in Allen."

***

Michele arrived with her mother and their baking supplies at the address given to her and after the quick introduction, she got busy in the kitchen of the Diarrassoubas. Mrs. Diarrassouba had a commercial oven for no other reason that her son entertained guests in his profession that often needed such an equipment to cater to his events. Soon, they were mixing flour, eggs, sugar, and butter. Within an hour, molds were already lined up and decorations ready to go. Mother and daughter were in sync and worked fast.

The theme of the *walimah* were navy blue, white and baby blue. So, the baking team made cupcakes with blue-leaf orchids and a decent five tower white cake with pearls. The top of each tower was decorated with layers of navy blue and baby blue. From the top to the bottom of the cake, a branch of blue orchid cascaded down. And at the top of cake, she put an ornament of two bedazzled intertwined hearts. When Afou saw the cake thirty minutes before the guests were due, she shrieked out of joy, "Dude! You a Cake Boss! Respect man! I knew you could pull it off."

Trying to hide her smile, Michele replied, "Don't forget you tried to get married behind my back."

"Sorry, come on, let us, my family dress and wrap you in our clothes," Afou said, very apologetic and hurriedly at the same time as she ushered them to a guest room so the last-minute guests could quickly clean up before the ceremony started.

Epilogue

The Katib

March/Ramadan

AFOU DECIDED SHE WILL cook with Charles once a week to build the habit again, and Charles agreed to accompany her to weekly *tazkiyyah* meetings at the local *masjid*. If they were not able to attend, they made it a point to watch the live or the recording together.

USCIS-F1 didn't get enacted as a policy but Choualiyou promised to keep trying especially in other municipalities. "This is my life's fight from now on," he told Afoussata. "Insha'Allah, Allah ﷻ will make a way," she replied as they were watching their weekly spiritual segment one day in Ramadan after their return from *umrah*, in his Dallas apartment. Hudhaifa was sitting in the middle of them.

"Insha'Allah," he said back to her smiling fondly. They had just finished eating *iftar,* and they were resting before going to pray *taraweeh* at the local *masjid*.

" The " true" servants of the Most Compassionate are

...

those who pray, "Our Lord! Bless us with " pious" spouses and offspring who will be the joy of our hearts, and make us models for the righteous. ".

– Quran 25:63-74

THE END.

BOOK THREE: THE CORD

" Be mindful of Allah and Allah will protect you. Be mindful of Allah and you will find Him in front of you. If you ask, then ask Allah [alone]; and if you seek help, then seek help from Allah [alone]. And know that if the nation were to gather together to benefit you with anything, they would not benefit you except with what Allah had already prescribed for you. And if they were to gather together to harm you with anything, they would not harm you except with what Allah had already prescribed against you. The pens have been lifted and the pages have dried."

– Hadith 19, 40 Hadith an-Nawawi

" The ˹true˺ servants of the Most Compassionate are

...

are˺ those who pray, "Our Lord! Bless us with ˹pious˺ spouses and offspring who will be the joy of our hearts, and make us models for the righteous."

– Quran 25:63-74

Table of Contents

Chapter 1

Azimatu

Shawwal plus one week

RAMADAN HAD JUST ENDED, though she was still on her period. Therefore, she hadn't been fasting for a while even though Azimatu observed everyday as if it was a day in Ramadan. She was always mindful of herself, her actions, and the people she kept around her.

Leaving her closet and fully dressed in a shiny emerald *jilbab* that went well with her radiant brown skin, Azimatu made her way to her prayer corner. Her petite form did not reveal the giddiness she felt just approaching it. Azimatu had made the small space the epitome of comfort and worship by selecting a prayer mat in lovely pink hues with matching plush pillows. She glanced at the clock on her phone and noted the time. It was almost 10:00 am. Azimatu whispered *"Bismillah"* and went unto *sujud* reciting more silent supplications and confessions to her Lord. She felt happy to regain this closure again, happy to report for duty. She felt the duty because she fully internalized that she was just created to worship Him ﷺ.

When she returned from *sujud,* she said *"Alhamdullilah"* and grabbed her French and Arabic Quran, diving right in, careful not to touch the Arabic letters since she was not in state of purity. Still, because she was a regularly reader of Quran, there was a *rukhsa* that allowed her to remain connected to the words of her Creator even when she wasn't tracing the *surahs* with her fingertips. Compared to Ramadan, when she read a *juz* or more per day, her current rhythm had slowed down to enjoying just a couple pages at each prayer time. Azimatu did this to still meet with her Lord even if she did *not* have to. It was easy to come to Allah ﷻ when the *adhan* reminded us to pray, but she had realized it was harder to think of Her Friend Allah ﷻ when she had her period and wasn't praying. With maturity, Azimatu realized that friendships are built on a lot of showing up. So Azimatu had perfected her consistency for fear of falling off the wagon and losing her anchoring routine.

Chapter 2

Majid

Shawwal plus one week

EVERY DOOR HE HAD knocked on this morning remained unanswered. So, Majid prayed for a door to open soon because the Texas heat was taking its toll on him on this bright summer day. Wearing ankle length loose blue jeans and a long sleeve cotton canari t-shirt, he was prepared for the weather. *Alhamdullilah ala kulli haal.* The water in his gourde had even warmed. Beads of sweat had started to appear on his face and soaking into his full groomed beard a bit. The next apartment on his list was on the first floor, so he appreciated a bit of shade while waiting for the renter to respond. A young man opened.

"Hi, I'm Majid. I'm with the US census for 2030. We are doing preliminary tests."

"Hi…" the teenager said, eying him curiously before blurting out, "Are you Moslem?"

"Yes," Majid replied and quickly changed the subject. "Are your parents in?"

"No. But I doubt they would want to talk to you. Maybe lose the Moslem hat. But between me and you, I dig your outfit. Some of my school acquaintances are Moslem."

"Hmm…When will they in?" Majid asked.

"Later today," the teenager replied.

Majid had no intention of changing or getting rid of his white kufi. When he took this job, the only condition he gave was that he would not enter people's houses. He didn't trust all people to let him out alive. The social and political climate was just too tense for him to risk going into an unfamiliar homes and possibly never coming out again! *Hasbun Allah w animal wakil* was his motto. What was written for him would not miss him but was not meant for him would definitely be averted by Allah ﷻ. Majid was positive of it. He said a low "*Alhamdullilah*" for the kid's warning tip.

Chapter 3

Azimatu

AZIMATU WAS READING A page in Surah Baqarah in her decided slow-paced *khatam* after Ramadan when there was a knock at the door. She cringed. Her son was out running an errand, so she knew she had to pause her reading to go open the door. Who could it be? She wasn't expecting anybody or any delivery. Azimatu finished the verse letting out an *astaghfirullah* and then headed out to the front door before impatience took a hold of the unexpected guest.

Before opening the door, she looked through the peephole and was aghast. Intrigued, she opened the door.

"How can I help you?"

"*Assalamu aleikum,* sister," Majid said instead, smiling. She noticed his little surprised look as well as some relief settling on him.

"*Wa aleikum salam,* brother. How can I help?" she repeated, a little more impatiently this time. Her whole body played a traitor in reacting to the beautiful sight of this man. She immediately knew why he affected her so much. She hadn't fasted much lately to press down her *nafs*, and she had not read Quran as much either. Her normal spiritual defenses against these things were extremely low. Her heart had been left unguarded due to a bit of her own laziness in wanting to take her *ibadah* easy these days. Azimatu mentally kicked herself. One of her teachers always said that a true *awliyyah* of Allah ﷻ completes a *khatam* weekly if not one *khatam every* ten days. That's about three *juzs* a day. It only took two hours max to finish a *juz* after all. He wasn't her only teacher who had alluded to that. Another of her Quran teachers said that a Hafiz of the Quran tries to read the entire Quran in six days on a continuous basis and that the seventh day is just to get back on track in case you fall off the wagon the sixth day. With her teaching job, she limited herself to a *juz* a day after work. We are supposed to live like it was Ramadan and that was feasible for her. She didn't respond to the interrupter right away. He stared at her a bit, taking her in before saying, "I'm Majid with US Census Bureau. Can I ask you a few questions?"

"I'm in the middle of something. Can you wait until my son comes back? I should be done with my recitation insha'Allah, too, by then."

"Sure."

"Do you want a cold bottle of water?"

"I would appreciate that," he eagerly accepted.

She closed the door behind her to grab a bottle of water. When she opened the door again, she was hit with another wave of feelings and emotions she couldn't canalize. Her lower self was too excited to the point of feeling sinful, and it shamed her. She lowered her gaze and handed him the bottle of water. He easily folded into a kneeled position in the *sunnah* way to drink. She tried her best not to look at him while he was removing the seal to bring the bottle to his mouth.

'*Astagfirullah*,' she repeated non-stop under her breath until she announced she needed to finish her task.

Chapter 4

Azimatu

AZIMATU RETURNED TO HER task, reading until her being was recentered. Not long after, she heard the front door open. Her son had returned from the store.

"*Assalamu aleikum,*" Mujahid extended to the house.

"*Wa aleikum salam waramatulahi wabarakatuhu* Habibi. Welcome back."

"Thanks. There is a guy sitting outside," he told Azimatu.

"Yes. I was waiting for you before I addressed him," Azimatu replied sighing with a heavy exhale.

"Why are you rolling your eyes, Mom?" her son asked with an intrigued smile, taken aback by her exasperation.

"Apparently, they started the census questionnaire for 2030 already."

"Isn't that a little too early?" he asked with a puzzled look.

"Don't ask me. I don't work there. Let's get it over with and release the man. It's hot outside."

"OK, let me put the groceries away," Mujahid said and got busy opening and closing pantry and fridge doors. Then, he washed his hands and led his mom outside. For a seventeen-year-old, he towered over his mom.

Once they were outside, it was Majid's cue to get up from the stairs he was sitting on, under the shade of the building. He approached the little family and Azimatu spoke first.

"*Assalamu aleikum* Brother Majid. This is my son Mujahid. We're ready for you."

"*Wa aleikum salam. Alhamdullilah.*" Majid answered and turned his full attention to Mujahid with a full smile.

"How are you young man?"

"I'm good *alhamdullilah*. Mom, should we bring chairs here; in front of the door?"

"No Habibi, we can go straight to the balcony from here." Without any words, she locked the front door behind her and led the way by taking about ten big steps to her right before lifting the latch granting access to her cozy and minimalistic decorated balcony. She lightly dusted her seat before sitting and said, "*Bismillah*. Please sit." Muhajid closed the small gate behind him.

"You must love green," Majid said, noticing the shades of green around him.

"I love all the colors of our Creator *alhamdullilah,*" she replied, *alhamdullilah*. Her *jilbab* was green but she also loved elegant *abayas* with rhinestones that didn't necessarily have to be green; just stylish and presentable.

"*Alhamdullilah*. In any case, I liked the view behind me when I took shade under the stairs. This is a very nice community grill you have there, surrounded by tall bougainvillea, trees, and other apartments buildings. I would have stood there for shade, but my legs were tired, so I sat."

"I agree with you. My balcony gives over a nice scenery, *masha'Allah alhamdullilah.*"

Chapter 5

Majid

"*ALHAMDULLILAH*. OK, LET'S start. I'm Majid Robinson, and my fun fact is that I'm originally from the Caribbean. I'm also a census employee, and I'm here to complete the preliminary steps we need to accomplish so that the 2030 census runs smoothly, *insha'Allah*. I will start with basic questions." He had added his origins just to break the ice and put them at ease.

Mother and son nodded. They got the jest of it.

"What's your name Sister and your marital status?" Majid asked. A part of him was eager to know these answers.

"I'm Azimatu Dosso, and I'm divorced."

Majid nodded and jotted that down.

"What's your full name Mujahid?" he asked, again turning and giving his full attention to the young man like he was trying to make a point. Majid himself didn't know if he was trying to impress the boy or assert himself to the boy. It was a mystery he wanted to solve for himself but he put it on the back burner for now.

"My full name is Mouhammad Mujahid Dosso. I go by *Mo Mujahid*," he specified.

"OK. Thanks for the detail. Now, are you originally from West Africa? And how long have you been living here?" he asked them both.

"Yes, we are. I came here over 23 years ago. He was born here. We plan to still be in the USA by 2030 if God wills." Azimatu replied.

After noting down everything, Majid said humming: "Interesting. My ancestors were from there; West Africa. My last name is not really Robinson; it's an adaptation of the West African name Sonko; meaning 'second born.' Since son of Robin, like Rabbi, is closer to that, my ancestors anglicized our original name to Robinson."

"That's very interesting," Mujahid pointed out.

Azimatu cocked her head, replying, "Really? *Rabbaniyyun. Masha'Allah alhamdullilah.* You learn new things every day."

"Spot on." Majid commented and continued asking more relevant questions about his task and mission.

Chapter 6

The Katib

Shawwal plus two weeks

AFTER MAJID INTERVIEWED AZIMATU and her son, he took her number. Every Jumu'ah, he would send her a simple message wishing her a blessed *jumu'ah mubarakah*. *Jumu'ah was* also the day that Azimatu connected with her crew on a WhatsApp thread named "The Muslimah Cougars." While Hajar lived in Dallas County, Azimatu lived in Denton County, and Afou lived in Collin County. Charles and Hajaratu moved out of his apartment in Uptown. The ironic thing about their pun-intended group name was that they had attended **Collin Community College** before it became **Collin College**. The school's mascot was a cougar. The friends had roomed with female basketball players, called The Lady Cougars. It was destiny that some twenty plus years later, they had finally become cougars in their own right. They were now older, attractive women in relationships with younger men. Or about to be.

Every *jumu'ah*, Hajar and Afou asked Azimatu if she had met someone new. They either caught up online or at their community center where a weekly Ivorian *khatirah* program was held.

The first *jumu'ah* after the census interview, Majid texted Azimatu. So, she looked forward to chatting with her sisters from the motherland and telling them about the encounter. The woman had easily formed a bond in Dallas's niche Ivorian community. They called their sisterly romance a "sro-mance." People who discovered the group's name found it very quirky. The sisters, however, believed it was a little brilliant.

That friday, when the first notification came in from Hajar saying, "*Assalamu aleikum Muslimah Cougars! Bon Djouman!* What's new Habibties?!" Azimatu jumped in her seat, her heart leaping with excitement. She was so ready to share her new secret.

"*Wa aleikum salam waramatullahi wabarakatuhu* habibties! Jumu'ah Mubarakah…I might have met someone…"

"What?! Spill the beans," playfully ordered Hajar. She was always the fastest texter in the group.

"*Salam*, yes! Tell us more," Afou also prodded impatiently. True and dear friends, they always matched each other's energy in the moment.

Azimatu recorded a voice message to explain.

"No, we need to see her face!" Afou insisted.

"Right, just for the record we need to see **Madame-I'm-OK-being-single**." Hajar sided with Afou and immediately initiated the video call.

"Hello? *Assalamu aleikum* sisters," Azimatu was giggling and uncontrollably lowering her gaze. She was not able to meet her friends' eyes which were amazingly both judging and sparkling with glee.

They continued teasing her. "A Mister Robinson! Look at the irony?!" Hajar noticed.

"Right? Everything was created in a pair even that name; the good connation--hopefully him since he is Rabbaniyyun. And the naughty connotation of Mrs. Robinson, the cougar from the movie *The Graduate*." Azimatu said, going on a philosophical tangent while ironing away invisible wrinkles on her pink satin *jilbab* with her hands. Her face was illuminous as usual, no doubt because of her daily recitation of the Quran.

"The only thing created in a pair that I'm interested in for you is the one from Surah Naba. I can't wait to see you with the man of your life!" said Afoussata, being tickled and serious at the same time.

"Allah سبحانه و تعالى has still blessed you with *nur* even if your *nafs* are considering this scandalous relationship!" Hajar added. "*Masha'Allah, alhamdullilah.*"

"*Astaghfirullah!*" Azimatu interjected, "It's not scandalous yet. My thoughts are a bit unpure sometimes at the thought of him, but when I see myself enjoying visions of us almost crossing the limits, I try to shut them down immediately."

"Subhannallah! How old is he?" Afou asked.

"He is thirty-five."

"Hmm, a young horse..." Afou concluded.

"A stud indeed. But we aren't helping her by adding more fuel to her desires." Hajar said more to Afou than to Azimatu.

"Thank you! I have not been active for years and my barriers against any desires are weak at the moment. I'm currently threading a very thin and

173

dangerous path. When I tell you my *nafs* are toying with me big time, they are. I block them in my sleep due to many years of perfecting and mastering closing the door to Shaytan, but now the imaginings just flash before my eyes while I'm wide awake. It's wild. Sometimes, I'm so overwhelmed by need that I find myself going along with the daydream before the sense to snap out of the reverie railroads me to WAKE UP!"

"May Allah سبحانه و تعالى help you control your desires for Majid, *aameen*." Afou prayed.

"*Aameen*," Hajar followed.

"*Aameen*! I seriously need it," Azimatu admitted.

"It's a test; indeed," Hajar agreed and recited ayah 2:155 from the Quran. "And only you will figure out how to pass...with or without Majid."

"Maybe. We will see. Insha'Allah." Azimatu said, exhaling deeply. "Well, I will invite him to the next *khatirah* if he is still around, and your husbands can sound him out insha'Allah."

"That's a wonderful idea if he can come." Afou said with palpable excitement in her words.

The friends talked more about their families, children, parents, work challenges, and their future vacations for nearly an hour before ending their chat.

Chapter 7

Azimatu

"*ASSALAMU ALEIKUM.*"   AZIMATU TEXTED Majid.

"*Wa aleikum salam waramatulahi wabarakatuhu* Sister Uzma."

She smiled at the way he liked to use her nickname. She found it endearing.

"Are you busy next Friday night?"

"Actually, I have plans."

"How about the Friday that follows?"

"I believe, I'm free. Why?"

"We have a small reminder in my native community, and I would like to invite you there. That way, you can meet my people and see our ways a bit, *insha'Allah*."

"Sure. I'll be happy to attend, *insha'Allah*."

***

The Katib

Shawwal plus 3 weeks

Two weeks passed and Azimatu and Majid were still checking on each other weekly. Every *jumu'ah* morning they exchanged platonic niceties about the blessed day ahead. They wanted to talk to each other daily, but they knew that doing so would open a door they might not be able to close. If they aren't careful, they would welcome in *zina*. Texting once a week was the safeguard Majid had implemented and Azimatu had silently endorsed. They were old enough to know the intricacies and pitfalls of wanting more interaction. Their *taqwa* made them realize that Allah سبحانه و تعالى is watching them every moment.

"How is Mo Mujahid?"

"He's good *alhamdullilah*. He's busy applying to colleges right now."

"I see. Does he know we talk?"

"Yes, I don't hide anything from my son."

"What does he think?"

"He's happy someone is interested in his mom. Talking of moms, tell me about your family."

"My parents live locally. They are good," Majid said and added, "They are non-Muslims."

"Have you told anyone in your circle of friends or family that you are talking to a single mom?"

"Way to ask the difficult questions right away!" he replied with a laughing and sweating emoji.

"I'm 41 years old and you are 35 years old. We have to address the elephant in the room," Azimatu replied not backing down. She didn't have time to waste.

"I'm working on finding a way to tell them as this continues to have legs, insha'Allah."

"Rabbani," she wrote, using the pet name she was set on for him, "Please don't take too long."

"OK, Sister Uzma."

The mood dampened after that, and they ended their playful chatting with *salams* and *duas* to one another.

Chapter 8

Majid

Dhul-Qadah

MAJID HAD ENJOYED AZIMATU's community and had returned to it a few times when he didn't have Friday plans with his buddies. He was regularly social in his own community as well as the Pakistani Muslim Community where he took his *shahada*.

At Majid's first *khatirah* in Azimatu's community, the *imam* talked about *istiqamah*; being constant, staying the course. Majid shelved the pearls of wisdom he benefited from and waited to be introduced to more friends and family, which wasn't too long after. Azimatu approached him to meet her relatives; her aunt and uncle, who were in their late sixties.

"*Assalamu aleikum* Uncle and Auntie." He greeted them politely.

"*Wa aleikum salam waramatulahi wabarakatuhu* young man. Welcome to our community." The couple replied. They aged well in their family, he internally noticed. Azimatu's relatives looked like they were in their mid-forties, *masha'Allah alhamdullilah*.

The eleventh-month had rolled in, and Majid was still placated on the manner to approach his family about the matter of Azimatu. He had seen Azimatu's mom on a video call one day when she called her mom who was visiting Ivory Coast. Azimatu briefly introduced him since they were sitting on her lovely balcony having a quick discussion about their relationship. He had stopped by after Magrib because he knew that a lot of misunderstandings happen with text messages and was worried. He was gone within an hour of arriving; her house rules. "I won't be known for a harlot around here," she explained. Since during the summer, the sun sets closer to 9 p.m., it was not too bad to receive him between 9 p.m. and 10 pm. He laughed at her choice of words.

Majid's conversion to Islam had been a point of contention in his family. And now this; his attraction to an older woman with a child. He had said no to many girls his mom Josephine had introduced him to. When she saw her plans failing, she started recruiting *hijabis*. As long as he started giving her grandchildren, she would swallow her disapproval of his new religion.

Majid did his best to call her and his father a couple times a week, mainly on Monday and Thursday nights before bedtime.

It was Thursday and Majid was dreading his regular call with his parents. He knew they would ask the hard questions, just like Azimatu did. He felt squeezed between them.

"Marcel, how are you son?" his mother asked on the other end of the receiver. She still called him by his non-Muslim name because it was hard to retrain her mind to call her son an odd name he hadn't picked for himself.

"I give thanks Mom. How are you Maman?"

"You know how I am. My eldest is still unmarried, and I have no grandchildren. I worry, and I'm worried I will never see my legacy in this life."

"Tell him again," his father chimed in the background. Marcel just closed his eyes and hung his head. He was so closed to lose it, but **he remembered** the advice given to him. When he was new to the faith, Majid regularly attended a convert care program to help him. It was especially useful to navigate the difficulties he faced with his blood relations. Listening to his mother, Majid recalled the advice **that patience is at the first try**. And that his character is what will perhaps attract his family to Islam, too. So, he did his best to not be short with them in any way, even if they irritated him on a constant basis and took jibes at him and his new faith, his beard, his outfits, his name, and the list went on.

Chapter 9

Majid

Dhul-Hijjah

MAÎTRE DIARRASSOUBA AND HIS wife
Afoussata had returned from *hajj*. The community
gathered at their residence to welcome them back
and celebrate the couple. Majid was invited since
the couple had met him at the Muslim Ivorian
Center who was just a room equipped with
beautiful rugs for now capable of containing 100
people. The *mihrab* area had been customized into
a niche with several layered beautiful rugs along
with a small bookshelf, a microphone, and some
Islamic art decorations to denote the prayer corner.
The experience was wild to him. West Africans
were vibrant people, like Caribbeans, but with a
touch of uniqueness that he fell in awe for. From
embroidered *bubu bazins* to lush *oud* smells, it was a
mind-blowing event.

Majid had been expecting a lunch served on a table
at the councilman's house. Nope! The couches of
the living room had been pushed to the corners of
the room and several rugs were laid on the tiled
floor. Men and women sat on opposite sides of the
room. The ceremony started with the name of
Allah ﷻ. Then, a small reminder was spoken,
followed by *duas* for the new *hujjaj*.

Finally, several plastic covers were placed on the rugs to protect them from the crumbs and any oil drops.

Following the lead of the men around him, Majid had washed his hands with soap and water, which was poured out for him from an ornate vessel right where he sat in the living room. The food was delicious. The host had served boiled yams with fried lamb meat. He loved the *daguaba*; the big round dishes of food that everyone communally ate from. Each big plate had a group of men huddled around it, eating voraciously with their hands. The delicious sauce accompanying the meat reminded him a bit of a Jamaican dish. When he was full, he licked his fingers and washed his hands like everyone else. From afar, he could tell that it was the same setting for the women. Azimatu was amongst them, and his heart flipped every time his eyes fell on her in the gathering.

At the end of the gastronomic segment, the hosts thanked their guests, and everyone leisurely dispersed. Majid waited outside to see if he could greet and talk to Uzma before leaving.

While waiting outside under the five-o'clock Texas sun, his eyesight fell on the small open shopping chic mall across the two large streets separating the gated community from the mundane life of Mckinney. Majid wasn't an obsessive shopper, so the name brands didn't faze him. What phased him was the romantic vibe of the area. It was an ideal spot for a casual stroll with a loved one. Large basins of water, fountains, colorful trees, pocket prairies and the like adorned the space, and he could easily spot them in the distance. Then an idea struck him.

"*Assalamu aleikum*, I'm outside. I want to see you before I leave. Better, I want to take a casual stroll with you across the street. We can digest the food we ate by the same token."

"Sure. I will be right out," was her speedy response.

Chapter 9

Majid

Muharram

AS THE ISLAMIC NEW Year ushered in, the community wished each other a happy new year and extended *duas* to one other for prosperity, high *eeman,* and long healthy lives. That month, it was Hajar and Tariq's turn to invite their friends over to break the fast with them in honor of Ashura. Falling on a weekday, the community agreed to commemorate the event the upcoming weekend.

Majid had been in different parts of the state because of his job. It allowed him to observe the characteristics of each city of North Texas. The part of town he had been invited to for Ashura dinner, Northpark in Uptown, was known for having many thick green trees and large castle-like dwellings. While there were also many chic and expensive townhomes in the area, his hosts lived on a quiet street with mailboxes lining it in front of each McMansion. A saying Majid had heard around the Ivorians popped into his mind while he took in his posh surrounding; *"Les moutons se promènent ensemble mais ils n'ont pas le même prix."* The lambs hang out together, but they don't have the same price. Before envy settled in his heart, he whispered; *"Masha'Allah!"* It was more to himself than anything else. He parked his car, adding it to the multitude of cars already in the driveways and along the road.

The host Tariq greeted Majid at the door.

"*Assalamu wa aleikum* Brother, please come in."

"*Wa aleikum salam,* thank you!" The other guests were already there. He joined the light conversation until *iftar* was served and then the host turned his attention to Majid.

"Did you check out that Islamic library in Richardson I recommended?" Tariq asked Majid.

"Yeah, it's vast, *subhannallah.* But I didn't find the book I was looking for there. That said, the librarian took the name of the book and will try to get it from his book dealer in Cairo, *insha'Allah.*"

"Perfect," Tariq replied, passing the pounded yam plate to Charles so he could serve himself.

"Thanks," said Choualiyou and then he passed the plate to Majid. Majid couldn't help what he said next addressing his host Tariq. "So, your chef cooks all the dishes?"

"On days he is out, I cook sometimes, or we eat leftovers from his previous batches," Tariq answered. He shrugged his shoulders and served himself a heaping portion of a tasty okra stew with a ladle filled with all types of meats: crab, *pgôlô* (beef skin), fish, and beef meat.

"Interesting," Majid pinned. Azimatu cleared her throat from the other end of the table where she was sitting with the other two women. And that was his cue to shut down that discussion. They exchanged an inaudible conversation with their eyes that everyone noticed, creating a brief moment

185

of awkwardness before they resumed the lively discussion around other mundane topics.

Chapter 10

Azimatu

Safar

MAJID'S MOTHER INVITED Azimatu for tea and was surprised to see that she wasn't dealing with a wrinkled woman.

"Because of *halal* food restrictions, I insist on coming only for afternoon tea so that I don't subject the elder woman to a lot of cooking. Plus, I'm very picky on what I consume. There is a high chance I won't like traditional Caribbean food right off the bat." Azimatu had pointed out to Majid after being informed of the invite.

"Women…" he shook his head. "I ate your food without any complaints," he said, looking a bit hurt by her words.

"I know Rabbani. But I don't look this young because I consume *everything*," she said, sweetly, batting her eyelashes at him. The *haram* police would have hanged her if they had witnessed this moment.

"Fine!" he grumbled, letting her win.

At his petite and greying mom's place which was at a cozy family home in Richardson, after the formal introduction, Majid's mother spoke while his tall and handsome father with the Nubian nose and darker skin tone just smiled. They were equally older, like Azimatu's relatives at the Ivorian *masjid*.

His parents were in their early seventies for sure, she concluded.

"Are you sure you aren't 26?" Majid's mother asked Azimatu, pleasantly surprised that her son's interest didn't look her age. Her biological clock was ticking but nobody had anything on her about her looks. Since she was non-Muslim, Majid knew he couldn't share a picture of Uzma with his mother or with other *non-mahrams* from the get-go. Azimatu smiled and all resistance dissipated here on out between his family and her.

After their successful first exchange, Majid's mother started supporting his relationship with Uzma. The only hurdle was the pressure she subjected them to; "Get married soon and get busy. I want my grandchildren!" Her comments made Azimatu, who was shy, lower her head and giggle uncontrollably like a girl. She focused her gaze on the rug facing her and whipped her head around from time around the room. They were seated in the *salon*; in the true French sense of the word. The open kitchen facing them led to the garage door. The house was a two-story house where the upstairs led to more rooms, bathrooms, and a game room. She passed them when she asked to use the restroom. The restroom downstairs was being used. And the only other one on the first floor was in the host's bedroom so she couldn't use that restroom. Azimatu finally noticed that the windows next to the salon that gave on the well-trimmed grass in the expansive backyard.

Chapter 11

The Khatib
Rabbi One

AZIMATU AND MAJID CONTINUED a low maintenance checking in on each other for six months until winter rolled in and brought along the seasons of parties. The local Arab *masjid* Azimatu attended had several appreciation events in honor of their regular donors. She was invited to many different dinners and had invited Majid to a donor appreciation event. Normally, she went alone or with her son. She was ecstatic because his presence would remove the attention of the other women from her. Lowkey or with overt aggression, most married women feared attractive and devoted single women like Azimatu in the Muslim community. Usually, she acted like she didn't notice their stares, microaggressions, or knowing looks. She simply kept her head down, ate, and talked to any cordial body at her table. This year, it would be different.

They non-couple arrived in different cars but sat at the same table.

"*Assalamu aleikum*, Sister Azimatu," he greeted her in the parking lot. His dashing smile matched his crisp thobe.

"*Wa aleikum salam waramatulahi, Brother* Majid. How are you doing on this wonderful chilly night?" she asked as he held open the door to her Mercedes Benz.

"*Alhamdullilah*, sister. Not bad. How are you dear sister?"

As they continued their niceties and small talk, more guests arrived and parked. Without dallying outside too much, because the cold air was too nippy, they quickly trudged inside. As soon as they stepped into the hall the sisters who knew her along with some nosey brothers had questioning looks on their faces.

'Are you surprised?' the look she flashed back asked. Not hiding a grin, she was satisfied that she was winning. At that same moment, Azimatu asked Allah سبحانه و تعالى to forgive her for the satisfaction she was feeling. *Ya Rabb! Help me not cross your boundaries, aameen.*

In the event room, most families and acquaintances huddled together around the same table.

"*Assalamu aleikum,* brother!" a man in the room zeroed in on them. "Did you finally steal one of the jewels of our community? We didn't hear about a marriage."

The question took Majid by surprise, but he was equally quick and sharp in his response.

"Well, she is off the market for sure. Brother...?"

"Brother Bashir! Nice to meet you Brother...?"

"Majid. My name is Majid."

Majid continued to field a lot of questions around his relationship with Azimatu. Some people even asked him straight up why he was interested in an older woman with a child. He continued to dodge them diplomatically without being concise in any responses.

Azimatu also received some landmines. What was the alternative way to deal with all the assumptions? Say that they were on a date? The community would collectively lose their minds because Azimatu and Majid knew better than to be on a date, especially at a mosque function! So, both smiled at each other's resourcefulness at dodging landmines and continued to enjoy their dinner.

Chapter 12

The Khatib
Rabi Two

AZIMATU TOLD MAJID TO get straight to the point. She asked him what he was looking for in a spouse. Majid's list was too traditional and somewhat naive for Azimatu because at this point in her life her devotion was her priority.

"Well, I want a spouse who can cook for me regularly. A wife who can clean and a wife who still rear children and manage our finances."

"Basically, you want a secretary," Azimatu cut in sharply as they were having a talk on her balcony one evening after they had a dinner, which she had managed to scramble up for them. Thankfully, the baked potatoes with colorful bell peppers along with the fried chicken with the spicy deep were easy enough to make, whip, and serve in a record's time. If there was one thing Azimatu hated besides idle time, it was long hours cooking in the kitchen. She saw long hours of cooking as a waste of time. Her budget of time principle in the kitchen is that she should never have to spend more than hour in the kitchen.

"It sounds bad when you put it that way Uzma. I know many people who don't see any issues with these tasks," Majid pointed out. His stance on a woman cooking for him was the reason they had "that eye talk" when Tariq mentioned his Chef or himself cooking for his wife Hajar. Azimatu blocked him from voicing his opinion that day to her friends. It wasn't the time for that.

"Hmm," is all she said and then added, "what time will I consecrate to my Lord if you are intent on eating my cooking all day every day? She was a dessert queen of no-baked goodies, but that didn't mean she enjoyed standing in the kitchen for long hours at length. Her son learned to cook at ten years old because he knew that his mom needed the constant watering of the Quran to love him. She needed a lot of pouring into her own cup to have the bandwidth to love him. Mo Mujahid made the correlation easily. If Mom had more time with Quran, she loved him more, but she had less time with Quran, she was on edge. Consequently, she was less affectionate towards him. So, he decided to do his part; help his Mom love him better. *Alhamdullilah.*

Back to the lovers, Majid continued to convince Azimatu to no avail for the umpteenth time until they switched to the topic of children for the umpteenth time as well. Majid was still prime to have children. And he wanted them as soon as possible. Azimatu wanted them but she had her reservations she didn't voice. Their relationship had become a landmine of touchy subjects she wished she could avoid at all costs.

While Azimatu was thin on love bandwidth with children, her two friends Hajar and Afou were busy lining up pregnancies. Hajar was in her second pregnancy after two years of marriage. Afou was also pregnant. Reflecting on their situations and knowing that she might be in their shoes on, it dawned on her that Allah سبحانه و تعالى perhaps blessed Khadijah رضي الله عنها with almost all the children of the Prophet ﷺ to show to people that older can have many children, too! The *azwaj mutahharah* were younger and logically the best bet for children bearing. But Allah decided only that Khadijah رضي الله عنها and the concubine will bear his ﷺ's children. That amazing realization awakened Azimatu and deepened her awe of Her Creator; *signs for people of thought indeed,* she inferred. Even the examples of Prophet Ibrahim and Zachariyah *aleihum salaam* were also great examples of old folks rearing children only His Might!

Snapping out of her reverie while standing in her kitchen, Azimatu reached out to the scented orchid vanilla hand soap bottle to get a dollop before bringing her hands to the faucet for a quick handwashing. She was stressed by love and babies, that she actually wanted to bake a cake to numb her racing mind with some baking math.

Chapter 13

Majid

Jumada One

MAJID SAW AZIMATU'S unwillingness to sacrifice for him as a lack of care and love for him. He was hurt. He said, "When you love someone, you don't make excuses. You simply do things for them. You learn their love language."

"You're right. I Love Allah سبحانه و تعالى more," Azimatu said, lowering her gaze. "Instead of wasting each other's time, let's do *istikhara* and take a compatibility test." She suggested.

Majid agreed and left her place somberly that night.

***

Azimatu

The next day on Friday, when she arrived home from a normal day of work, she quickly washed her hands as usual and directly turned her longing to her Lord like surah 94 verse 8 advises. She read the Quran and did some *adhkar*. When Azimatu felt a bit calm, she pulled out her diary and started logging a love letter. It was an emotionally-charged love letter she knew he would never read.

Majiiid, she wrote with the inaudible moan resonating in her own head. *Majiid.* She repeated the sensual moan in her head again. She did that again and again until she was satisfied. *Ugh! You drive me insane*, she finally whispered on the brink of ecstasy and climax. *Every bit of me is yearning for your touch, for your kisses, for your full attention. I have imagined hajj and umrah with you. It's so vivid in my mind that I deny the fact that it can't be real. I have also imagined sweet and tender love in your arms. I have imagined your warm embrace around me even if we have never hugged. The point is I can't imagine a life with another man. When I meet or see a man who can fit the profile I am looking for, I make myself lower my gaze and ask Allah سبحانه و تعالى to only make my eyes for you. Wild, right? I don't even know why I continue to make such duas when it's clearly not working out at the moment between us. That doesn't stop me from desiring you though. I am powerless Majid. Powerless. I am having a hard time turning off my lower-self.*

Majid
Jumada Two

Azimatu had once used a delivery service for a tray of mango mousse Majid had ordered. So, after releasing her deepest emotions on paper again like customary lately the day before to take the pressure off, she decided to pay him a visit in his lair. Her conscience warned her that it was seeking trouble and foolish, but she ignored the voices. We behave ourselves in my place all along, insha'Allah it will be fine. So, she went ready to confront him and make him understand her side of the story. It was a Saturday morning and she knew he would be home. Majid lived in a decent gated community where he rented a room in a family house with other tenants. When she arrived there, Azimatu knew she had been there. She wracked her mind to try to remember when until it hit. One of her hot dreams she had recently, had been a place like that. She had even forgotten it. Now, it came like a punch to her heart. She clearly remembered how he deliberately kissed her in her dream, and she didn't stop him. When they were they satisfied of the passionate kiss, they exchanged some words she couldn't remember and took vacancy of each other's companies! *Subhanallah, our souls met! Allahu Akbar. You should turn around before it becomes reality,* a voice in her warned. She dismissed it and proceeded to knock at his main door. A tenant she didn't know opened and she explained her business there.

"Hi there, I'm here to see Majid."

He looked at her curiously and said, "you mean Marcel?"

"Huh?"

"You look Muslim. The only Muslim tenant here is Marcel. Hold on, let me go get him," he said and closed the door gently.

"OK…"

A few minutes later, Majid emerged surprised. "What brings you here?"

"Can we speak privately?" she asked.

"Of course. Come in"

She followed him to his bedroom. She immediately noticed how half a wall divided his bed was from his personal sitting area. His wooden queen bed was made with grey and white sheets. A bedside commode took domicile one side of the bed with a chic black lamp posing on it. His cellphone, keys, and wallet kept company to the tall lamp, besides it. On the other side of the half-wall in his room studio, there was a small sitting arrangement of three comfy chairs and an average size flat screen TV on which a match of soccer followed its course.

"Have a seat," he offered and Azimatu sat.

After Majid sat, she cleared her throat and launched into a tale.

"My parents had a beautiful marriage until my father passed away. So, I always wanted something like their love, dedication, and commitment. I thought I had found that in my very traditional ex. My ex-husband lied to me about money, about his previous marriage, about a lot of things. I was devoted to him. I cooked. I cleaned. I sacrificed my career for him until all his lies caught up to us and it was a bitter pill to swallow. So, I swore I would never serve a man like that again. And that I would prioritize my relationship with God first. I blamed myself for putting a creation before the Creator. This is why I'm the way I'm. Why aren't you married at your age?"

"Coming from the background I come, we date before committing. My parents were high school sweethearts. They didn't get married until they finished college. Once I became Muslim, I cut off all ties with her because she didn't want to follow me in my new religion or make it *halal* for me. *I am very principled*, and the choice was clear."

"Masha'Allah," she complimented. "We aren't that different."

199

"I agree."

"I dreamed that we kissed," she said and stared at Majid to see his reaction.

His mouth made an "o" first. Then he squinted. Next he asked, "did you like it?"

"Very much," she confessed, lowering her gaze. "I need to go," she said, getting up abruptly, eyes still on the floor. But she found him right in her face, chest heaving.

"I did, too. But it was a bit involved," he let out with a voice thick with need.

While her eyes were wide with alert, his eyes stared at her tempting lips she just wetted with her tongue before swallowing hard. She took a step hard and quick backed away while reciting "*audhu billahi mina shaytanir rajiim.*" Truly, the third person in their gathering was Shaytan. But ultimately, she knew their Lord, the Watchful, was also in attendance. So, her feet carried her as fast as possible out of the trap she willingly walked in while Majid stood there dumbfounded.

Chapter 14

The Katib

Rajab

SO, MAJID AND AZIMATU took a compatibility test. They were compatible for the most part *masha'Allah alhamdullilah* except for the spousal duties and children rearing parts. And this wasn't a surprise to either of them. This was the part they were advised to work on if they wanted their relationship to have any legs to stand on and succeed.

In the end, Azimatu and Majid tried to talk to an Imam to try to find common ground with their diverging views on spousal duties. In the end, the Imam gave them both a verdict.

"Brother Majid, Sister Azimatu is not required to serve you. It's commendable if she does but it seems she has other priorities, and you are not at the top of those priorities even if she deeply cares for you. May Allah سبحانه و تعالى help you find the perfect fit. *Aameen.* This match is right *masha'Allah,* but it's not perfect," he said, looking at the pained face Azimatu displayed.

She always said, "Love is not enough."

"Sister Azimatu, may Allah سبحانه و تعالى make it easy for you, too." Azimatu nodded, unable to voice any words.

The Khatib
Shaban

The month of Shaban that year was agonizing for our lovebirds. Majid and Azimatu had stopped communicating because of their differences. The first week, Azimatu really missed seeing Majid at the Monday *halaqas* of her local *masjid*. That night she went to bed heart shredded and broken. She was still hopeful of seeing him later during the week. However, he also didn't show up at the Friday's circle of her Ivorian community weekly get together. Early that Jumu'ah, she had patiently awaited his regular "blessed jumu'ah" message accompanied with *duas*. She waited in vain for the message to materialize itself. For the first time in her life, she was annoyed when the Cougars' well-wishing messages came in. She was deflecting her anger, and she knew it. Through it she upheld her normal character and behaved as she should. *Astaghfirullah*, she said to herself later. Look at how this man is making react to my friends. *Subhanallah!* It scared her.

One week went that way with no sign of life from Majid. It was suddenly harder to navigate her daily life without his presence. However, at each *salah* time, Azimatu managed to put her worldly desires asides.

She truly shed them for the numerous meetings she had with her Lord daily for she always exhaled deeply and said before any *salah*, "Ya Allah, help me forgot *dunya* and only focus on you," as she lifted her hands just above her chest ready to let the *takbir* and start her office time with Allah سبحانه و تعالى. For the promise of seeing His face one day, she numbed her feelings and prayed each prayer as it was her only shot. She tried to have *Ihsan* in her worship; by worshipping Allah سبحانه و تعالى as she could see His Majestic face. But if she couldn't see Him سبحانه و تعالى, Azimatu knew He سبحانه و تعالى saw her because He is al Khabeer.

One more week went by, and Azimatu was doing her best to keep it together. Her girlfriends checked in on her.

"How are Habibty?" they had asked.

"One day at a time. I will be fine insha'Allah."

"May Allah سبحانه و تعالى grant you patience and ease," Hajar and Afou prayed for her.

"*Aameen*, thank you Cougars," Azimatu replied with a half-smile, and they all busted out laughing, lightening the mood for a moment.

The month ended with Azimatu praying to Allah سبحانه و تعالى to show her the way; to ease the cracks in her soul. Soon, she started getting used to his absence with a lot doing and accepting the consequences of the choices she had made. Since she had lived through a separation with her first marriage, the verses of the Quran that tells the believer that He knows that the situation of divorce hurts but to still stand up and pray to Him hit her quite daily during this difficult time for *salah* is supposed to be a moment of relief, peace, a connection to our Lord to fill our cup with His Divine Love and Light. It was the gift Allah ﷺ gave the Prophet Muhammad ﷺ after the year of sorrow during *isra wa-l miraj*.

The Khatib

Shaban

After the initial shock of the "selfishness" of Azimatu settled in, Majid became very sad. He didn't want go to work for a couple days. Kowing himself, he didn't want to be found walking aimlessly in the streets of Dallas and being hit by a car as a result because he was out of it. So, he called in sick. Sick with love. The first person he had called was his Mom.

"Maman, can you believe it? She doesn't want to cater to a man anymore because she is busy praying the majority of the time!"

"While I want to hang her for it, the Lord comes first my son," his mother said tactfully.

"Which side are you on Mamam?!"

"Yours of course! But she has a valid point."

Majid made a disapproving clucking sound and requested to talk to his father. His father just listened to him and in the end said, "Son, it will be OK. You will make it."

Not feeling their support at all, Majid did his best to not lose his temper with them and ended the call with them.

After three days of mopping around his apartment while struggling to get his *salah* in at each appointment, anger and feelings of confrontation sparked in his heart. This was enough to fuel his muscles to return back to work. Majid stayed mad like for another week. He didn't call his parents because he felt like they betrayed him and because he wanted some space. He tried to hang out with his *masjid* crew and decent non-Muslim friends he still had to forget the sting. Fearing they would react like his parents did, he didn't bring up the issue to them. Besides, how was he going to explain the relationship without it coming up like a *haram* relationship since there is no dating in Islam. Azimatu and him weren't married. They didn't cross any intimate no-no because of their *taqwa* but nobody would understand that they could control themselves because they didn't want to disgrace themselves and take away the favors He ﷻ had bestowed upon them. They knew better than to trade Allah's closeness for a fleeting moment of flesh.

When his feeling of anger finally subsided, sadness took a hold of him again. It's then he realized that he hadn't told the Being he needed to bring the issue to all along because he was busy with his ego. So, when the realization hit him, he went straight in *sujud* and said, "Ya Allah, I have wronged myself. If you don't forgive me, I will certainly be of the wrongdoers. Ya Allah, I love your beloved servant Azimatu. However, I think she is a bit over the top with her worship. Please incline her heart to make time for me if you decide to join me in holy matrimony with her. Ya Allah please. Ya Allah I have no need or intention to compete with You. I will never win this fight. Ya Allah, I just want her as my cover and I want to be her cover. *Astaghfirullah*. Please answer my *duas*, please don't return my hands empty Ya Rabb, *aameen*."

Chapter 15

Azimatu
Ramadan

At last, Azimatu concluded that she was well off without a man. Yes, she missed a man's attention and warmth. However, the man who will not mind her long reading sessions of Quran, her daily *hifz*, and her continuous seeking of knowledge had not come to her doorstep yet. So, for now, she would do her best to remove Majid from her system. His sight enflamed her whole being so much that it scared her. *I will not follow my desires. Ya Allah, help me curb this desire,* she prayed and went in *sujud* sobbing. *Everyday is Ramadan for me…*

After that prayer, it felt like a bug bit her. Azimatu was suddenly energized by a message from Majid.

"I can cook and clean. Can you please meet half-way? Meet you at your door in an hour."

Azimatu smiled and started cleaning her apartment like a tornado in reverse. Majid never sat for too long in her living room, but she acted like he was sleeping over. She agonized over the fact that he might need to use the bathroom and it would be dirty. And that she had no snacks to offer him in case he was hungry! She had no idea how a 180 flip had occurred in her. *Allah*…her mind suggested…*Al Musawwir, the changer of Hearts.* "*Alhamdullilah,*" is all she whispered as she bounced

207

off the walls of her apartment straightening poofs and shoving dishes into the dishwasher. It was *ajib*,

Epilogue

MAJID ASKED FOR AZIMATU's hand in marriage, and she accepted. Then, he asked her for the proper way to proceed with her family. She explained that the elder uncle of the family of her father needs to be informed. So, they both traveled to go meet her mother so he could show his respects to the mother of the bride. It was early spring, so Majid wore his trademarks ankle-length loose jeans with a pink shirt this time around, a Sebago, and a white kufi. Azimatu switched it up a bit by wearing an elegant fuchsia Ankara print dress with a purple *hijab*.

The flight was about four hours. He was a stress ball, and she kept reassuring him.

"Relax, it will go well *insha'Allah*."

When they landed, they made their way to baggage claim to recuperate their luggage. Her sister and her brother were supposed to pick them up. When they safely boarded the car, Azimatu introduced her sister Naima and her brother Mustapha to Majid. They hit off right away *alhamdullilah*. While they conversed, he admired this new state; a bit old in its architecture but majestic in its own right. He enjoyed the greenery though which wildly contrasted with Texas. Besides, the license plates of all the drivers read: The Garden State.

It will be jannah--paradise insha'Allah after this meeting is over. He told quietly to himself.

209

Forty minutes later, they pulled up at the residence of the mother of the bride. Majid dropped his carry-on. He was still very nervous to meet someone who was stronger in character than Azimatu. He could barely handle Azimatu...he tsked laughingly at himself. *Ya Allah, please make it easy.* He silently prayed.

***

They were shown their separate rooms. They cleaned up a bit, prayed and ate. Then, they called for a meeting with the head of household and the mother of the siblings; Lady Fatima.

"It's nice to officially meet you, Mom."

"Likewise, my son. I have heard a lot of good things about you. And I have seen a lot of good signs, too *masha'Allah alhamdullilah*. Welcome to the family. I will call her uncles from her father's side and give you a number you and your family will need to contact." Azimatu's mom said as they were sitting in her living room in Newark, New Jersey.

"No problem Mom," Majid agreed ecstatic. He had the blessings of the mother of Azimatu and *insha'Allah* they will be on a good start.

When all the logistics were set up, Azimatu and Majid traveled to Ivory Coast to perform the actual ceremony. It was cheaper to perform it overseas. Their friends who were younger professionals were also able to attend. They just had to cover their ticket prices and lodging, pictures, and food would be covered. Azimatu and Majid pitched in so that his parents and some of his important relatives in the islands could travel to attend the wedding in the county of the bride. Then, the next plan was to have the honeymoon in his country, The Dominican Republic, in the Caribbean islands.

***

The Mandingue Wedding
The Katib

Azimatu, Majid, and their American guests departed from the United States on Sunday night from New York Laguardia Airport and arrived in Ivory Coast on Monday; the next day around 11 a.m. Azimatu's cousin Ben picked them up from Abidjan International Airport Félix Houphouët Boigny in a white van. Ben then made stops at seven uncles and aunties places; Uncle Mohammed and his wife housed a groomsmen and bridesmaid. Then, Auntie Anta received another set of groomsmen and bridesmaids. So did Auntie Muna and her husband, Uncle Amr and his wife, Uncle Souley, Uncle Ousmane and his wife, and finally Uncle Hakim and his wife. Majid and Mo Mujahid were dropped by Ben at Auntie Aicha's House. Auntie Aicha was the direct paternal aunt of Azimatu.

When Majid's parents arrived later that day, they were lodged with Azimatu's side of the family that was non-Muslim. They would be mainly attending the *walimah* at the hotel and watching the religious

211

ceremony via Zoom along with other relatives who couldn't attend the *nikkah* in person.

Azimatu herself stayed in her mother's house with her mom and many of her close relatives.

Azimatu's friends Hajaratu and Afoussatou were not among the bridesmaids, they were the *débah*— the sponsors of the weddings. They had their special outfits and categories compared to the bridesmaids and groomsmen. Since they also had family and relatives in Ivory Coast, they stayed with their relatives.

Majid's friends and their pairs included Ahmed and Nuha, Sanaa and Azimatu's son, Koubra and Marwan, Yusef and Sheefa, Amina and Ubaydillah, Mustapha and Rokya, and finally Philipe and Maria.

They rested well all of Tuesday and called a meeting in order at the main family home in Williamsville; the family headquarters to finalize the last details of the wedding with the family and the local wedding planner they hired.

By the same token, they got to greet the majority of the family. Then, the next day, the festivities began with the *mise en chambre* of the bride at her mother's house. That Wednesday night, Azimatu's feet and hands were decorated with *henna* by the qualified women of her community. On Thursday, the *henna* paste was removed, and she was instructed to make *ghusl* and wear a specific type of cloth print intended just for the bride along with a white *hijab*. The fabric is shiny and indigo based, a specialty clothing originally from her tribe's people. This outfit is given away to the main person who takes care of the bride in her room. An older woman by the name of Samira was catering to Azimatu. So, she would be receiving the beautiful outfit as a token of appreciation before the mosque's ceremony.

Then, the bride is brought into the living room where guests and well-wishers come to greet her, congratulate her, laud her character, eat, sing melodious traditional acapellas, dance, and provide a good ambiance in all.

When this step is over, the bride returns to her room again. In early traditions, she remained there for three days and wasn't allowed to speak; until Saturday or Sunday when the traditional ceremony took place. In recent years and more adhering to Islam circles, the bride, the groom, and everybody else got ready to go to the *masjid* to perform and witness the *nikkah* ceremony on Thursday after *zhur salah*.

For the *nikkah*, Azimatu wore a beautiful white dress made of cotton *bazin* fabric with a white *hijab*. Majid also wore the same white fabric. The mosque was packed with guests from all over the city and from far and between who either knew Azimatu's mom, Azimatu or anybody related to the bride or groom. African weddings usually didn't have a set guest list. People attended on their own volution and right. And you couldn't turn down anybody because they didn't rsvp. *Alhamdullilah ala kulli haal.*

The uniform agreed upon for the event was a purple UNIWAX print, and the colors of the wedding were purple and beige. Family members were free to buy the print and tailor it anyway they saw fit; as long as the whole family was on the same wavelength at the wedding events.

So, the groomsmen wore purple suits, beige undershirts, black ties, pants, and shoes.

The bridesmaids wore purple abayas with shiny rhinestones with a beige *hijab*.

Hajar and Afoussata wore very beautiful embroidered purple *bazins* with *hijabs* that had layers of purple and beige.

After the ceremony started, the imam gave guidance and tips to both the groom and the bride because culturally, only the woman is advised and cautioned to obey her husband while the man is left to his own devices resulting in a lot of marital disagreements in the community in the long run. Newer imams were proactive in cautioning both men and women of their duties. He also cautioned the witnesses to also do their part because they will be asked one day. When his sermon was over, he asked the questions all the guests were mainly there to witness.

"Do you accept to take Azimatu as a wife?" the imam asked Majid in French.

"I accept!" Majid replied, loudly. And the crowd roared with approval. Then, the imam addressed the wife to be.

"Sister Azimatu Awa, do you accept to take Brother Majid.P as a husband?"

"I accept!" she enthusiastically replied, and more applauses, whistles, and roars erupted from the attendees. The imam gave them the marriage licenses to sign. Their witnesses signed too, and the imam concluded the ceremony with heartfelt *duas* and well wishes *duas* for the new couple.

Majid.P and Azimatu Awa looked at each other at last with big smiles radiating on their faces. They could now do that without feeling guilty or feeling like they were transgressing. *Alhamdullilah*.

From that point on, the loud festivities were on full blast with the *djélis*—female griots entertaining the guests at the *masjid* and on the way to the hotel where the *walimah* will take place while pictures were being taken throughout.

Nuptial Night
Azimatu

After cutting the cake, eating, and enjoying the atmosphere with her groom Majid at their table, she was accompanied by her sisters, relatives, friends and cousins to the couple's room at the hotel away from prying ears and nosy minds. After uncontrollable giggles and words of congratulations, her crew left her. The bridesmaids informed the groomsmen to walk Majid to the designated room.

She had groomed herself for months for this encounter she had been waiting for, for years *subhanAllah*. She had treated her afro hair and had her teeth cleaned. Azimatu even made herself a full body curry and coffee mask to remove dark spots on her elbows, between her legs and knees. Azimatu really looked forward to blowing her groom's mind on their first night and many nights after.

215

Majid

"This is your night man!" said his best friend and best man Ahmed in their main hotel gathering room. "Say 'Ya Mutakabir' before anything. *Insha'Allah* you will be successful and have a great child from this night."

The rest of the six groomsmen burst out laughing. One even added, "Our marabout is back!"

"Shut up! My Sheikh gave me this tip to say before intimacy," Ahmed teased back, sure and proud of himself.

"We don't doubt you." The men replied.

"Enough everyone. Thank you for the tips. It's much appreciated. Take me to my bride so I can see if it really works," Majid prodded, laughing. So, without any further delay, they took him to his bride.

The Katib

When Majid knocked at their hotel room door, Azimatu's heart raced, and panic took a hold of her. So, she made a prayer to calm her nerves.

"Come in," she yelled out. Majid swiped his card and entered the room. He was dressed in a white *bubu bazin* with the matching *kufi* embroidered in the same intricate detail as the tunic.

"*Assalamu aleikum*," he extended to her as she sat by the edge of the bed waiting for him.

216

"*Wa aleikum salam* Habibi," she replied, casting her head down.

Majid quickly closed the distance between them and sat next to her. Then he leaned toward her and kissed her cheek. She turned her head and faced him; her eyes hooded with love and passion.

"Let's take our time," she whispered, her eyes focused on his lips.

Majid nodded and words were no longer necessary. They started communicating with her eyes and hands. She stood up in the dimly lit room, and he followed suit. Azimatu reached out to the hem of his tunic and lifted it over his head. He in turn delicately unpinned her *hijab*, letting her hair free from the headscarf.

"Wow!" he exclaimed to the bouncy afro curls that he freed.

"I hope you like natural sisters," she said coyly.

"I heard they are crazy picky, but I can live with that." He put his hand through her well-treated curls.

"They will become hard tomorrow but tonight they will behave *insha'Allah*," Azimatu pointed out as Majid's amazement continued.

From her hair, his hand slid down her back to unzip her white *bazin* dress. Within a few minutes, they were out of their traditional outfits and staring at each other. Majid was left in just his boxer and Azimatu was in her beige bras and pants. Then, a pull simultaneously drew them closer, and they started kissing slowly while exploring each other's bodies with hungry, discovering, and explorative

217

soft hands. Majid groaned at her touch while she moaned in delight from his electrifying touch.

They enjoyed each other from that point on until they reached the peak of their love making; climaxing beautifully together; locked in each other arms; sweaty and satisfied. Smiling at each other, staring deeply into each other's souls.

"Round two?" they asked in unison like they did when they wanted to serve each other more delicious food.

"Of course!" was their response like they did on the table when they ate. And round two was on and the many next rounds that followed until they collapsed from fatigue in each other's arms hoping they didn't miss *fajr*.

☪

THE END.

"Ramadan, the Sultan of Months. And the month of true love for Allah ﷻ and His Beloved Messenger ﷺ."— *Fofky*